Bride's Bay Event Board

TODAY'S SCHEDULE—
CONFERENCE ROOM

JURY DELIBERATIONS

PLEASE DO NOT DISTURB!

GUEST REGISTER

Talia Sagourin—Was she singled out for murder?

Cade Hailey—He didn't want to fall in love!

Joey Carpaccio—Was Talia on his hit list?

Bud Kendrick—Was he really looking out for the jurors?

Harlan Gates—Was he dangerous?

Myron Beyers—The jury foreman wasn't doing his job.

Roger Podonyi—Was the sharpshooter a hired gun?

The Mole—He could be anyone.

Love and Lies

Dawn Stewardson

Harlequin Books

TORONTO • NEW YORK • LONDON
AMSTERDAM • PARIS • SYDNEY • HAMBURG
STOCKHOLM • ATHENS • TOKYO • MILAN
MADRID • WARSAW • BUDAPEST • AUCKLAND

To Julianne Moore and Marsha Zinberg,
my two terrific editors for this book, with thanks for
inviting me to be part of the Bride's Bay series.

And to John, always.

ISBN 0-373-22362-5

LOVE AND LIES

Dear Reader,

For a woman who lives in a country that's covered in snow several months a year, I seem to have written a lot of books set in far warmer climes—from Mexico to Arizona to Georgia to the Dominican Republic.

At any rate, when I was asked to write a book for the Bride's Bay series, with its South Carolina setting, I was delighted. So there I was, the snow swirling outside my office window, writing a scene set on a moonlit beach on a sultry spring evening. (Now, is that a great example of escapism, or what?)

Of course, it's the characters, rather than the setting, that make a story, and in the case of *Love and Lies* I really came to admire Talia Sagourin and Cade Hailey as I wrote about them. Thrown into a potentially deadly situation, they toughed it out—and fell in love along the way. I hope you enjoy reading their story.

Warmest regards,

Dawn Stewardson

P.S. If you're ever in Charleston, be sure to take the ferry over to Jermain's Island. You never know what adventure might be waiting there just for you.

ABOUT THE AUTHOR

Dawn Stewardson is the award-winning author of over twenty novels for Harlequin. "A few years ago," she told us, "I served on a jury. At the time, I hoped the experience would someday prove helpful in writing a book, and *Love and Lies* turned out to be that book."

Dawn lives in Toronto, with her husband and a small menagerie of pets. Their turn-of-the-century house was built by a retired sea captain, and she's certain it has an intrigue somewhere in its past. She keeps hoping to find buried gold in the garden, but so far has found only bones the dogs persist in burying.

Books by Dawn Stewardson

Chapter One

His stomach felt sour—a combination of nerves, the stale antiseptic smell in the washroom and the desire to be just about anywhere else on earth. He'd known, though, that he'd end up having to meet Joey Carpaccio's goon somewhere in the courthouse.

There hadn't been a prayer all the jurors would vote not guilty the first time around. Hell, they'd even been instructed to bring a suitcase with them this morning, just in case. And he'd known that once the voting was over they'd be stuck here until they were sequestered—and that Carpaccio wanted to hear, right away, the details of how the vote had gone.

But knowing he'd had no choice about things didn't make him feel any better. And he was going to feel a lot worse if one of the other jurors walked in here. Or the court officer. Anxiously he glanced toward the stall Joey's goon had disappeared into, wondering how long he was going to be.

The guy was a casting director's dream—a perfect movie gangster. So if any of the others caught the two of them in here talking, it wouldn't take Einstein to figure that whatever was going on shouldn't be.

Telling himself to relax, he glanced at his reflection in the mirror and smoothed his hair, deciding he looked as sick as he felt. He was as pale as a mole living in a burrow—a good analogy, considering he was a mole on the jury. Joey Carpaccio's secret eyes and ears.

Not willing eyes and ears, though. If he could have turned down the money he would have. But that hadn't really been an option. He'd gotten more an ultimatum than an offer. Finally the toilet flushed and the goon reappeared, his newspaper still in his hand.

"At least it ain't gonna be in the papers every day now," he muttered, shoving the morning's *Charleston Times-Courier* under the mole's nose.

He read the most recent headline: CLOSING ARGUMENTS IN CARPACCIO TRIAL THIS MORNING.

The jurors had been instructed to avoid newspapers, along with radio and TV news about the trial, but this was far from the first of the coverage he'd seen. Even if he'd wanted to go along with the instructions it would have been impossible.

A lot of people still took Charleston's nickname of the Holy City seriously. So when a married woman was shot to death while in bed with her lover it had been front-page news for days. And when her wealthy club-owner husband, with his rumored mob connections, was charged with the murder, the ensuing trial had been news from beginning to end.

"So whaddaya think about our problem?" the goon demanded. "How's it lookin'?"

"I'm not sure. I told you, it was a secret ballot."

"But she voted guilty, didn't she. She hadda be one of the three."

The mole nodded. "I'm sure she was. But she could change her mind. The others, too. That's why they sequester us. So we talk about it until we all agree."

"So, who were the other two?"

"I don't know. As I keep telling you, it was a secret vote. But tomorrow, once we start deliberating, it should be obvious."

The goon muttered again—under his breath this time—but the mole had a pretty good idea what he was saying. He figured the jurors should have been talking, right from the start of the trial, about whether or not they thought Joey Carpaccio was guilty. That wasn't the way it worked, though. They'd been ordered not to discuss the evidence until they'd heard it all.

Tossing his newspaper into the trash, Joey's goon fixed the mole with a gangster stare. "The two guys, they'll come around. Whoever they are, we figure they'll change their minds. But what about the broad? You gonna be able to change her vote?"

"I'll do my best."

"Yeah? Well, see you do your *very* best. That's what you got paid for. And we don't wanna have to start worryin' about goin' some other route."

"Hey, lighten up." The mole was beginning to sweat. He didn't like that *we* he'd just heard. It sounded as if it might include him. And he didn't like that reference to some other route, either.

Taking a payoff to ensure Carpaccio didn't get convicted could land him in big-time trouble. But if Joey's goon started figuring he should help some other way... Hell, that could lead to worse trouble still.

He forced a grin. "We can't reach a verdict till all of us agree. And I'll hold out till Christmas if I have to. So what's the worst that can happen? Even if she doesn't come around, the worst thing possible's a deadlocked jury and a retrial."

"Yeah? Well, we don't want no retrial, see? We want this over and done with. We want twelve votes of not guilty. 'Cause if we go through this again, we might not be so *lucky* with the jury that gets picked. So we're countin' on you to deliver. And don't go forgettin' South Carolina's a death-penalty state, huh? That's makin' the boss real nervous."

The mole wiped his brow. The goon was making *him* nervous, and he didn't even want to think about what would happen if he *couldn't* deliver.

"And what's the deal with this resort?" the goon asked. "This Bride's Bay place? I never heard of a jury bein' sent off to some ritzy island."

"It was just the luck of the draw. They told us a retired judge's wife owns the place. And the old guy puts up a jury or two in the off-season every year—says he likes to give something back to the legal system."

"So's this ain't gonna screw up the plan, is it?" the goon asked. "You can still send stuff on your computer from an island?"

The mole nodded, thanking his lucky stars for that. Sending information to an E-mail address would be a hell of a lot easier on his nerves than more face-to-face meetings like this.

"You sure? Here." The goon pressed a slip of paper into the mole's hand. "Take this number. And if there's a problem and you gotta call me, do it. Just watch what phone you use."

The mole pocketed the number, assuring the goon everything was going to be fine. "I've got my cell phone right here in my briefcase," he said, "along with my laptop. So I won't have to use the hotel lines for anything. And," he added, giving the case a pat, "I won't let this out of my sight until we're there."

"Till you're there on your ritzy island," the goon muttered.

"It's probably not *that* ritzy."

"No? Well that's not what I hear. And where the hell does this old guy get off stickin' his nose in? I mean, he puts the jury up in a place like that, and you guys might like it so much you'll just settle in and enjoy yourselves—while the boss sits in jail worryin'."

"No. No, I don't think that'll happen." At least *he* sure wasn't going to enjoy himself. Especially not if he was reading that damn Talia Sagourin woman right, if there was no way she'd be changing her vote.

TALIA PAUSED on the veranda of the main hotel building, thinking how much her parents would love this place. They were history buffs, and Bride's Bay could be a picture from a history book—a photo titled *Afternoon at the Old Plantation House.*

The place was pristine white, with gracious columns on the verandah that supported a second-story wraparound balcony. And the grounds stretching away on either side were manicured to perfection.

"The whole island looks like a set from *Gone With the Wind,*" she murmured to Cade.

He smiled. "I don't recall Tara being surrounded by sand dunes and an ocean."

"Well, maybe not the *whole* island," she admitted, glancing back in the direction they'd walked.

It was far enough into April that the centuries-old live oaks were the succulent green of spring. And the Spanish moss dripping from their huge branches added to Talia's sense of the trees being rooted in time—in generations past, when many of the Sea Islands had been working plantations.

"Come on," Cade said. "Let's go get checked in."

When they stepped inside, Talia paused again, deciding that whoever had transformed the plantation house into a hotel had possessed a magic touch. The lobby exuded Southern charm—a gleaming wood floor, pale yellow walls with white trim, floor-to-ceiling windows and a sweeping staircase she could easily imagine Scarlett coming down.

"Too bad the circumstances aren't different," Cade said.

Talia nodded, her vision of Scarlett vanishing and her thoughts turning to the reason they were here. Tomorrow morning they'd start considering all the evidence they'd heard about Maria Carpaccio's death. And something felt unseemly, felt almost ghoulish, in fact, about coming to one of the most beautiful island resorts on the East Coast to deliberate over a murder.

"Thought I'd lost you two," their court officer said, materializing beside them. "Everyone who took the minivans up from the ferry has already checked in."

"We wanted to look around a little," Cade told him.

"And it's quite the place, huh? Didn't I say I was getting you in somewhere great?"

Talia shot Cade a surreptitious smile. To hear Bud Kendrick talk—and he was a gossipy sort, which meant they'd heard him talk a lot during the course of the trial—you'd think that he was in charge of South Carolina's entire jury system. And that the system would be at risk of total collapse when he retired next year. In reality his job as court officer consisted of looking after an endless series of Charleston juries.

One of the fellows on theirs had been quick to dub him Bud the baby-sitter.

"The whole island is really something," he was saying. "Even the north end, the section the Jermain family sold off way back when, is as exclusive as the resort. There are only twelve of those private estates I was telling you about. Just those, and the little village and marina."

Talia nodded. Bud had drawn their attention to the village marina when the ferry had passed it. It was where the estate owners kept their yachts and had things delivered from the mainland.

"And just wait," he continued, "till you have a chance to *really* look around. The place has everything from a championship golf course to the best shooting range I've ever used. I love coming here. Just wish I could afford to come as a guest."

As Bud talked, he dug into his pocket, produced a key and handed it to Cade. "You're sharing with Harlan Gates, and both the keys were in the same envelope so he gave me yours. It's room 227 and you can just go on up. You don't need anyone to show you the way.

"Now you, Talia, you'll have to get your key at the desk. Looks like Liz Jermain is on duty today." Bud gestured toward an attractive thirty-something woman. "She'll take good care of you. It's her grandmother who owns the place, but it's Liz who runs it. So, I'll probably see you both at dinner," he concluded, heading off.

"Well...guess I'll go check out my room," Cade said.

His gaze held Talia's for a moment longer than necessary, making her pulse give one of those funny little skips she was almost getting used to. Being chosen as a juror for a murder trial had to be the most improbable way on earth to meet an attractive man. But Cade Hailey was living proof it could happen.

The first moment she'd seen his rugged good looks, the first time his warm gray eyes had caught her gaze, she'd felt a stirring inside. And all the time they'd spend together over the course of the trial had only nurtured her initial interest.

They'd been together all day long, five days a week, for the entire six weeks. Yet even though she was sure the attraction was mutual, they hadn't done a thing about it—because there'd been absolutely no chance for them to be alone together. The jurors had been told not to fraternize outside the building. And inside the court building, all twelve of them had been there.

They'd sat in the jury box while the evidence was being presented and in the jury room during breaks. They'd drunk morning coffee together, eaten lunch together, and talked about a thousand and one topics. They'd done virtually everything but sleep together.

Sleep together. Talia looked at Cade once more and watched him striding up the stairs. He'd told her he was divorced, but hadn't gone into the details, and she'd long ago begun to wonder how any woman in her right mind could have let him get away.

She allowed her eyes to drift from his broad shoulders down the lean length of his legs. He was a construction engineer who owned a renovations company, and even if he hadn't told her that he enjoyed doing some of the physical labor himself, she'd have guessed.

Cade Hailey was, in awfully good shape. And he looked awfully good in tight jeans—coming *or* going. Watching him was enough to make her pulse skip again. She followed him with her eyes until he reached the top of the stairs, then she walked over to the desk.

"I'm Talia Sagourin," she told Liz Jermain. "One of the jurors."

"Yes, of course." Liz smiled. "The lone female. They only let us know which jury would be coming a couple of hours ago. But as soon as they faxed us the list of names, I began wondering how it would feel to be in your shoes—sequestered with eleven men."

"Well, it was a long trial, so I've gotten used to being the only woman."

"And at least it's getting you a room to yourself. I have you in 203, so I'll just—"

"Excuse me?" a woman interrupted.

Talia glanced at her, recognizing her from the ferry. Apart from the jurors and Bud, she'd been the sole passenger coming over from Charleston. About forty-five, she positively reeked of money.

"There's a problem with the room you gave me," she informed Liz.

A bellman in his mid-sixties—bell *captain,* Talia mentally corrected herself, glancing at the Bride's Bay badge on his uniform—had followed the woman to the desk. He shot Liz a look that said the problem was with the woman, not with the room.

"It's blue," the woman went on, "which is a color I absolutely loathe. Your man here had barely unlocked the door before I felt depressed. You'll have to put me somewhere else."

"Mrs. Wertman," Liz said, "I'm terribly sorry, but that's the only room available. It's not often we're fully booked before Memorial Day, but I'm afraid—"

"Let me speak to the manager," Mrs. Wertman snapped.

"I *am* the manager," Liz replied evenly. "And—"

Talia cleared her throat. Liz looked at her. Mrs. Wertman simply continued glaring at Liz.

"I have no problem with blue," Talia said. "So if 203 is a different color, I'd be happy to switch." Which wasn't to say she was happy about rewarding Mrs. Wertman's rudeness, but the woman was obviously going to give Liz Jermain a hard time if she didn't get what she wanted.

Liz gave Talia a grateful smile, then turned her attention back to Mrs. Wertman. "Room 203 is peach. Will that be satisfactory?"

"It's certainly better than blue. I find that such a cold depressing color," she added, glancing at Talia.

"But I'm glad it doesn't bother you. Thank you for changing with me."

"Shadroe," Liz said, "will you show both our guests to their rooms?"

The bell captain nodded, then led the way across the lobby and up the stairs. Talia half expected Mrs. Wertman to complain about the lack of an elevator, but she didn't. She simply walked in majestic silence the entire way to 203.

"I hope this is more to your taste, Mrs. Wertman." The bell captain unlocked the door and opened it for her.

Mrs. Wertman stepped inside, pronounced the room a vast improvement, then handed him a tip.

"Thank you, ma'am," he said. "Your luggage should be up shortly. But if there's any delay, you call downstairs and ask for me personally. My name is Shadroe Teach."

When Mrs. Wertman nodded and closed the door, Shadroe turned to Talia. And then he winked at her. She almost laughed out loud. She'd suspected there was a sense of humor lurking beneath his uniform, because he didn't quite look the part of bell captain at an exclusive resort. In fact, with his weathered face, curly white hair and heavy mustache, he looked more like an old pirate.

They started off again, and as they continued down the hall, Talia absently admired the large antique pieces of furniture that had been used to decorate it.

"We're just about there," Shadroe told her when they turned down another hallway. "The blue room is number 225 and I'm sure you'll like it. It's actually nicer than 203. It gets the morning sun, and there's a better view of the ocean from its balcony. So if the day's warm you can have morning coffee out there and—"

A piercing scream stopped him midsentence.

AFTER THE SCREAM DIED, there was nothing but silence.

"That didn't sound like anyone joking around, did it," Shadroe finally said, Talia's uneasiness mirrored on his face. "I think it must have come from Mrs. Wertman's room, and I'd better check on it."

He turned and began hurrying back the way they'd come, Talia trailing after him. A couple of doors opened as they passed them, and one of the guests came out into the hall. When they reached 203, there was no response to Shadroe's knock.

"Mrs. Wertman?" he called. "Mrs. Wertman? Is everything all right in there? Oh, my God," he whispered as the silence lengthened, "what's happened?" Fumbling in his pocket, he pulled out a ring of keys and stuck one into the keyhole. Then, with a final knock, he turned the door handle.

Talia held her breath, wanting to see into the room, but almost afraid to look. When Shadroe opened the door, though, nothing appeared out of the ordinary.

He stepped inside, loudly calling Mrs. Wertman's name again, and Talia followed him.

The room was luxurious, with enough space for both an enormous canopied bed and a large sitting area. Beyond that, French doors led to the balcony. They were fully open, and the sheers covering them were billowing ghostlike in the breeze.

"This," Shadroe whispered, reaching for the handle of a door on their right, "leads to the adjoining room." He turned the handle. "It's locked, so she didn't leave that way. And the far door's just the bathroom."

Talia looked past the mirrored closets, noting that the bathroom door was ajar an inch or two. Then she glanced toward the balcony again, murmuring, "Maybe she stepped out for a little air."

"She should have heard me call from out there, but we'll have a look."

Shadroe turned back toward the hallway and assured the guest who was trying to peer in that everything was fine. Then he closed the door and they headed for the balcony. There was no one out there, but Talia could see two obvious ways off it. The drop to the ground was only twelve or thirteen feet. And the walls that separated the balcony from those of the adjoining rooms hadn't been built with privacy in mind. They were only a little more than waist high.

But Talia couldn't imagine Mrs. Wertman either going balcony hopping or climbing over the railing and dropping to the ground below.

When she said that to Shadroe, he replied, "No. So where is she?"

Talia swallowed hard. He knew as well as she did there was only one place left to look. And Mrs. Wertman should have heard him call from in there, too. The door hadn't even been tightly closed. "The bathroom?" she suggested uneasily.

"You'd better wait out here," Shadroe told her, stepping back into the room.

Talia ignored his advice and followed on his heels. But when he called Mrs. Wertman's name a final time, then pushed the bathroom door fully open, she desperately wished she'd stayed on the balcony.

The trial photos of Maria Carpaccio's body had been gruesome enough. This, though, was the real thing. Mrs. Wertman was lying on the bathroom floor. In a spreading pool of blood.

Chapter Two

Shadroe Teach might have closed the bathroom door, but an image of the body in all its gory vividness continued to hover before Talia's eyes.

And she knew thoughts of it were bothering Shadroe, too. There wasn't much doubt, given the way he was pacing Mrs. Wertman's room. Or, more accurately, the *late* Mrs. Wertman's room. He'd established the woman was dead before he'd called down to the desk for Liz Jermain and spoken with someone from security.

Dead. The word kept echoing in Talia's mind, and every time it did her throat went dry. If she hadn't offered to trade rooms, she wouldn't be sitting here now on this love seat in room 203. She'd be lying shot through the heart on the bathroom floor, because she'd have been the one to walk in on the killer.

She tried to stop thinking about that by focusing on Liz, who was still on the phone. The manager's first call had been to ask someone to find Cameron Bradshaw, who, she'd explained, was her grandmother's husband and a retired judge. Now she was on the phone to the mainland, reporting Mrs. Wertman's murder to the police. She answered a few more questions, then finally hung up.

"Living on an island has its disadvantages," she said, looking over at Talia. "We're within the jurisdiction of the county sheriff's department, but their people have to get here courtesy of the Charleston Harbor Police, so it's going to take a while. And as far as hotel security goes, they've gone on red alert but the timing couldn't be worse. Our chief of security resigned last week, and his assistant doesn't have nearly enough experience for something like this."

Turning her attention to Shadroe, she said, "Shad? When you heard the scream . . . how long was it after you'd left Mrs. Wertman?"

"Not more than a couple of minutes."

"Then whoever killed her must have already been in here when she arrived. And hid in the bathroom when he heard the three of you at the door. Does that sound right?"

Talia nodded. "It would explain why she didn't scream right away."

"Exactly. She didn't see him until she went into the bathroom."

Talia's gaze flickered uneasily to the bathroom door. The next few times she walked into a bathroom, she'd be feeling more than a little anxious.

"But why did he hide?" Liz asked. "He obviously left by the balcony, so why didn't he take off as soon as he heard someone?"

"He probably panicked," Talia said. "Which would also account for the murder. I know that sounds extreme, but some people instinctively react to fear with aggression—the same way some dogs do."

When Liz looked at her curiously, Talia shrugged. "Understanding why people behave the way they do is my profession. I'm a psychologist."

"Well . . . I guess you should know then. But something about simple panic just doesn't sit right with me."

"Why not?" Shadroe asked.

"I think it's that you heard the scream but not the shots, which has to mean there was a silencer on the gun. Does that seem strange to you two? Or do most people who carry guns use silencers?"

Shadroe said he didn't have a clue, and Talia didn't know the answer either. All she knew was they hadn't heard any shots, but Mrs. Wertman had three bullet holes in her chest.

"We won't be able to keep this quiet," Liz was saying to Shadroe. "Not once the sheriff's people arrive. So how do we tell the guests? Lord, none of my hotel management courses even touched on how to cope with a murder."

"Don't you worry," Shadroe told her. "The Judge will know what to do."

As if he'd been outside waiting for his cue, a man tapped on the door and walked in. He had a kind grandfatherly face and gray hair that badly needed combing. His stained khaki pants were held up by braces, his well-worn sneakers had big knots in the laces, and the gray cardigan he was wearing over his checkered shirt looked as old as he did. All in all, if Talia had seen him under different circumstances she'd have taken him for a retired gardener rather than a retired judge.

Liz introduced them, adding, "Talia is one of our jurors."

"Ah." He smiled, then turned his attention to Liz. "What's the problem?"

She shook her head, as if not sure how to tell him, then came straight out with it. "A guest was just murdered. She walked in on somebody—a thief, I guess—and he shot her. Her body's in the bathroom."

"Well... that certainly *is* a problem. And she was also a juror, I take it? Rooming with Talia?"

"No, she wasn't a juror. Talia was simply with Shad when he found the body. Both Mrs. Wertman and Talia had just checked in, and Shad was taking Talia to her room when they heard a scream."

"Well, this isn't good," the Judge murmured. "But thank heavens at least your grandmother is away. If she hadn't picked this week to go and visit her brother... Well, homicide isn't something she'd enjoy having to deal with. I remember when I was presiding over a murder trial she'd get upset if I mentioned a word about it. So a murder right here in the hotel...well, I guess I'd best have a look." He crossed the room, then paused at the bathroom door and glanced back. "You *have* called the authorities, Liz?"

"Yes. And Shad notified security. They're watching for anything suspicious."

The Judge nodded, then gingerly opened the bathroom door and gazed in. "Did someone check for a pulse?" he asked, glancing back again. "Just in case?"

"I did," Shadroe told him. "And she's graveyard dead, Judge."

"I see. In that case, I'll just close this door again. The police don't like their crime scenes tampered with. They aren't even going to like the fact we've all been in here, so perhaps I'll call the sheriff and explain the situation to him personally. But before I do, someone had best tell me the particulars. Shad?"

The Judge listened intently while Shadroe repeated the same details he'd told Liz.

"Hmm," the old man said when the story was finished.

"Hmm what?" Liz asked.

"Well...I'm not so sure about your idea that the fellow was a thief. It doesn't take a thief long to realize a hotel room is unoccupied. So unless it was just a case of incredibly bad timing..."

"Yes?" Liz prompted.

"Well, it seems to me there's another obvious hypothesis. Perhaps he was waiting in here specifically to kill Mrs. Wertman."

"Oh, I don't think—"

"Don't be so quick to rule it out, Liz. He could easily have established what room you'd be putting her in, then come in and waited for her to arrive."

"No, that just can't be it, because this isn't the room I intended for her. I switched her and Talia at the last second. This was supposed to have been Talia's room."

"Oh," the Judge murmured.

Talia looked at him, suddenly cold all over. If his obvious hypothesis was right, the killer hadn't been waiting for Mrs. Wertman. He'd been waiting for her.

TALIA HESITATED when Shad Teach opened the door of room 225 and handed her the key. The last time she'd walked into a room there'd been a dead body in it. What if, this time, there was a live murderer?

"Don't you be worrying," Shad said. "The Judge is always coming up with his own private theories about things. He says when something unusual happens, people should consider all the possibilities and shouldn't just accept the obvious. Says they should ask themselves if what seems obvious is necessarily the truth."

She forced a smile. "And what do *you* say, Shad?"

"I say what seems obvious usually *is* the truth. So there's no sense worrying about all those other possibilities. What we had was a thief who panicked, right?''

"I hope so," she murmured. Unfortunately, though, the Judge had a point. Their thief theory might have been the obvious one, but that hardly guaranteed it was right. And when it came to the possibility someone might have intended to murder her rather than Mrs. Wertman, it was darned hard not to worry.

"Why don't I have a quick look around?" Shad suggested. "Just make sure housekeeping hasn't slipped up on anything."

Knowing he really meant he'd just make sure there wasn't a killer hiding in the bathroom, she waited in the doorway while he slid the closet doors open, checked the bathroom and stuck his head out onto the balcony.

Her suitcases, she noted, had been delivered to the room, but she didn't feel the slightest desire to go in and unpack. In fact, if she had any choice in the matter, she and her luggage would be on the next ferry back to Charleston.

"See?" Shad headed over to the door. "Everything's fine. The Judge got you scared for nothing. But look, if anything worries you, just call downstairs and ask for me personally. I'll come right up."

"Thank you," she said, trying not to remember that the last person he'd told to call down and ask for him personally had been dead before she'd had time to call anyone.

When Talia began searching in her purse for a tip, Shad motioned her not to bother and started back down the hall. Which meant she had to go into the room.

She tried telling herself it was a most inviting shade of blue. And that it was every bit as beautifully furnished as the peach room. Plus, it had the bonus—as Shad had promised—of a better ocean view. She could get a glimpse of the water from where she was standing, so she should go inside and have a good look. Besides, she could hardly spend the rest of her life in this doorway.

Just as she forced her feet to start moving, the door to the room beside hers opened. A moment later Cade Hailey walked out into the hall and smiled at her. It made her feel as if the sun had suddenly appeared from behind the clouds.

"There you are," he said. "I stopped by the desk a few minutes ago and discovered we're next-door neighbors. But when I tried knocking there was no answer."

"No, I was . . . delayed getting here."

"Oh. Well, I've been looking around, and there's a terrific bar. Why don't we go have a quiet drink before dinner?"

"Sounds like a good idea." Actually it sounded like a great idea. She wasn't much of a drinker, but she could sure use one at the moment. And she could also use a little of Cade's company. If anything on earth was going to take her mind off what had happened, being with him was it.

"See you later, Harlan," he called into his room. Then he closed the door on the sound of Geraldo Rivera shouting about something and gave her a look that said he wasn't exactly thrilled to be rooming with Harlan Gates.

It was easy to understand why. Harlan was in his early thirties, the same as Cade, but that was probably the only thing they had in common.

Cade had lived alone since his divorce, ran his own business and spent most of his leisure time outdoors. Harlan both lived and worked with his mother. They ran a motel on the outskirts of Charleston, and aside from that his only interest in life seemed to be computers. He'd brought a laptop along to the trial every day, often playing with it during breaks, rather than socializing with the other jurors.

"At least Harlan's pretty quiet," she said when she finally thought of something positive.

"Maybe he doesn't talk much," Cade muttered as they started down the hall, "but that doesn't mean he's pretty quiet. Did you notice he brought a printer along? As well as his laptop?"

"Uh-huh." He'd sat on the ferry with both items tucked safely between his legs—watching over them like a mother duck watching over her ducklings.

"Well, when the printer's doing its thing it sounds like a slow machine gun. And whether it's going or not, he's got the TV on full blast. Then he sits with one eye on the tube and the other on the screen of his laptop. And every time there's a commercial, he stops keyboarding and starts channel surfing. We're going to have to establish some ground rules, or he'll drive me crazy."

Talia laughed, but she'd been only half concentrating on what Cade was saying. Her attention had been straying to each of the decorative armoires and chests in the hall. Earlier she'd been admiring them. Now they struck her as ideal hiding places for a murderer.

"You said you got delayed," Cade reminded her as they started down the stairs. "Did Bud the baby-sitter corner you with one of his stories?"

Didn't she just wish that was all it had been. She shook her head. "I'll tell you about it when we get to the bar."

The Judge and Liz had asked her not to say anything about the murder until the sheriff's people arrived—so the guests wouldn't panic at the thought of a killer loose on the island. But Cade wasn't the type to panic. And telling him was hardly the same as shouting the news from her balcony. Besides, she had to tell someone for the sake of her own mental health.

When they reached the bottom of the stairs, though, she began having second thoughts. Liz and the Judge were standing right there, huddled in conversation, and the glance Liz gave her was definitely meant as a reminder to keep quiet.

She managed a reassuring smile and introduced them to Cade. Then, after the four of them had exchanged a few pleasantries, Cade steered her across the lobby and into a bar that looked as if it belonged in a private men's club.

Its walls were the color of sage; the old-fashioned couches and wing chairs were covered in dark green leather. And the draperies, which were shutting out most of the late-afternoon light, were exactly the same shade of deep green velvet as the ones Scarlett had fashioned into a dress. The bartender, who nodded a greeting from behind the bar, was a good-looking black man of about fifty.

"I talked to him for a few minutes," Cade said, "while I was scoping things out. His name's Desmond, and he grew up here on the island. He was telling me some really interesting things about it. For example, there are a couple of ancient tunnels leading from the cellar downstairs."

"Really? I didn't know you could have tunnels on islands."

Cade shrugged. "They'd just have to be well supported. At any rate, Desmond's lived here most of his life. Says he intends to die here."

"Mmm," Talia murmured, leaving it at that. She didn't want to think about anyone else dying here. One person had been more than enough.

THE BARTENDER SET Cade's glass of beer on the low table in front of the couch, along with the mint julep he'd recommended Talia try.

"I hope you enjoy it," he told her. "I grow the mint myself."

The smile she gave him was strained, and it added to Cade's sense something was very wrong. Normally Talia was easy to talk to. And she had a quirky sense of humor he really got a kick out of. But since he'd found her standing in her doorway, she'd been acting as if her best friend had just died.

He took a sip of beer, then sat back and watched her absently fiddle with her coaster. He liked looking at her, even though he knew it was about as smart as looking at a dish of ice cream while you were on a diet. But hell, any man in his right mind would like looking at Talia.

Her long tangle of sun-streaked hair framed a face that belonged in some upscale magazine. Her smooth skin was lightly tanned, her eyes a gorgeous deep blue, her cheekbones high and pronounced and her features regular—except for her mouth. She had the fullest, most luscious mouth he'd ever seen. All in all, it was tough to believe she was thirty years old and still single. Apparently, though, the right man had just never come along.

"You were going to tell me," he said at last, "why you took forever getting to your room."

Instead of telling him, she tasted her drink.

He tried not to begin staring at her lips again, but that proved to be like trying not to eat another spoonful of ice cream after you'd broken down and eaten the first one. There was something about her mouth that...

Well, it had made him start dreaming of kissing her before the trial had even gone into its second week—which, under normal circumstances would have had him running for the hills. The last thing he'd ever do was let himself get involved with another beautiful woman, because he'd seen firsthand what happened when the honeymoon was over and a beautiful woman began missing all the male attention she was used to getting.

But the way things were in this situation, he hadn't been able to run. He'd been forced to spend six entire weeks in close proximity to Talia Sagourin. Of course, he'd admit that he hadn't exactly been forced to sit beside her at lunch every day. Or spend the breaks with her. But when she'd turned out to be fun, on top of gorgeous...

"Cade," she said, finally looking at him, "something happened when I was on the way to my room. I'm not supposed to talk about it yet. The Judge and Liz didn't want any of the other guests knowing for a while. But I need to tell someone."

He nodded. Then, while he waited for her to continue, he let himself go back to just looking at her.

After all, there was really no reason to worry about being attracted to her. Hell, all he had to do was keep on playing look-but-don't-touch for however long they were at Bride's Bay. Then, once the deliberations were finished, once she wasn't right there in front of him day in and day out, he'd have no problem at all.

"Did you hear a scream?" she asked at last. "Not long after you went upstairs?"

"No, but when I got to the room Harlan was in the shower and the TV was on. Between it and the water running, I wouldn't have heard anything short of a bomb going off. But what happened?"

She glanced over to where the bartender was busily polishing a glass, then leaned a little closer to Cade. Close enough that he could smell her perfume. Its elusive scent made him think of a secluded stretch of beach on a warm starry night. And it made playing his game of look-but-don't-touch just a little trickier.

"A woman was murdered," Talia said quietly. "That woman who came over on the ferry with us."

Her words banished every thought of secluded beaches and starry nights, and he suddenly understood why she'd turned quiet and serious. He put down his beer and listened to her story. When she finished he ordered a second mint julep for her and a double Jack Daniels on the rocks for himself.

He was having one hell of a time thinking past the possibility she could have been dead now rather than here with him. And he needed something a lot stronger than another beer to help him cope with how much that possibility upset him. Maybe there'd been more danger in spending so much time with her than he'd realized.

The bartender arrived with their fresh drinks, and once he left Cade downed a slug of the bourbon. Then he got straight to what was worrying him most. "This theory of the Judge's... that it might not have been a thief..."

"You mean his theory it might have been someone waiting in there to kill *me*," Talia said bluntly.

Cade took another gulp of his drink. "That's just not... There's no reason someone might have been... is there?"

She stared down at the table.

"Well?" he pressed. "Is there?"

"Probably not."

"What do you mean, *probably* not?"

"I mean..."

She looked up and gazed at him with those big blue eyes, making his heart skip a couple of beats.

"From the moment the Judge raised the possibility," she murmured, "I've been asking myself. if maybe someone does have a reason."

"And?"

"And I have an overactive imagination. So I sometimes get way off base wondering about things."

"Things like what? Specifically in this case, I mean."

"Cade...do you think Joey Carpaccio might rather have me dead than deliberating his fate?"

Chapter Three

Did Joey Carpaccio want Talia dead? Cade sat rubbing his jaw and thinking there wasn't nearly enough Jack Daniels left in his glass. After hearing that question he could do with an entire bottle.

He wanted to keep thinking straight, though, so he didn't even glance toward the bar. Instead, he tried to decide if she could be onto the truth, if those three bullets really had been meant for her—courtesy of the accused. The thought made his chest feel strangely hollow.

Joey Carpaccio wasn't a man you'd want against you. His rumored mob connections were undoubtedly a whole lot more than rumors, and the guy was a murderer—guilty as charged. He'd had the best lawyers money could buy, but even they hadn't been able to come up with a credible defense.

Oh, not that he'd killed his wife himself. He had an airtight alibi for the evening of the murder, and the prosecution had never accused him of actually being the shooter. But they'd sure put together a strong case for his having planned the killing. And if he'd arranged for one death, why not two?

"Joey's lawyers didn't want me on the jury, you know," Talia said, breaking the silence. "You didn't sit in on much of the jury selection because you were the first one accepted, but they had a lot of potential women jurors excused."

"I realized they must have. I guess they figured the odds were better on men being sympathetic."

She smiled wanly. "By sympathetic, should I assume you mean they'd relate to Joey's situation more easily than women would? Relate to a man's murdering his wife because she was unfaithful?"

"Well...yeah." Cade drained the last few drops of his bourbon. This conversation was hitting a little close to home. He could relate, too damn well, to a guy whose wife had cheated on him. Even so, he couldn't see letting Joey get away with murder.

That put Cade in the minority, though. Only three jurors had voted guilty after the morning's closing arguments. He had. So had Talia, she'd told him afterward. He wasn't sure who the other one was, but he'd been surprised there were only three of them.

The way he saw it, the defense's unknown-intruder theory was a total crock. There was no way he'd believe someone with a gun had just happened into the Carpaccio house while Maria Carpaccio and her lover were in bed. But most of the jurors were obviously willing to give Joey the benefit of the doubt—whether his defense was lame or not.

"The only reason I ended up being accepted," Talia was saying, "is that they'd run out of peremptory challenges before they questioned me. So they had to either accept me or come up with a good reason I might be biased, and they didn't."

Cade nodded, wondering if the way she seemed to be adding things up actually made sense. He'd buy the fact Joey's lawyers hadn't wanted her on the jury. But it was a long leap from that to the idea Joey had arranged for someone to kill her. And she *had* admitted to an overactive imagination.

"If Joey was so worried about you," he finally asked, "why would he have waited till now to try something? Why didn't he get his friends to take care of it while the trial was under way? I mean, you live alone, so surely it would've been easy enough to..." He stopped speaking when he realized he was only making her more upset.

"That occurred to me, too," she murmured. "But I figure if anything had happened during the trial, the police would've suspected Joey was behind it. So maybe he was just hoping we'd all vote not guilty."

"If he actually thought we would, it would make him quite the optimist."

"Well, regardless of that, maybe when we didn't acquit him he decided getting rid of me had become critical. No matter whether the police suspected him or not."

"But he couldn't have been sure which way you voted."

"I think he'd have made a pretty good guess, don't you? Especially if...oh, Cade, here goes my imagination again, but what if he was concerned about me and had his friends do some poking around?"

He waited for her to go on, curious about what she was worried Joey's friends might have found. He hadn't suspected her of having any deep dark secrets in her past.

"Would they have come up with something interesting?" he finally said.

Talia nodded. "There's something his lawyers missed during the jury selection. When they questioned me, they asked about my practice, but they didn't think to ask if I take on any *pro bono* projects. If they had I'd have had to tell them I do volunteer counseling at a shelter called Safe Haven."

"A shelter? For the homeless?"

"No, it's a shelter for battered women. And if Joey's lawyers had known I do work there, I'm sure they'd have gotten me disqualified. They'd have claimed that since Joey was accused of killing his wife... Well, you see what I'm getting at."

Cade sat back on the couch, deciding maybe it wasn't really such a long leap to the idea that Joey had arranged for someone to kill her.

"And if his lawyers had claimed you couldn't be impartial," he said at last, "would they have been right?"

"I don't think so, although it's a question I wrestled with at the time. I thought I could be fair, but I kept wondering if I was only fooling myself. Because

I really didn't want to be disqualified, not when they'd been so blatantly stacking the jury with men.

"And now that the trial's over, I honestly think it was just hearing the evidence that made me certain Joey's guilty. I'm sure nothing else influenced me."

Cade nodded. The evidence had convinced him, too, so why not her? When he glanced at her again she was looking past him—across the bar. He followed the direction of her gaze and saw that a man of about forty had come in. Of average height and build, with short brown hair, he was wearing a dark suit and a deadly serious expression. He didn't look like a hotel guest in search of a drink.

He headed over to where they were sitting. "Ms. Talia Sagourin?"

Talia nodded.

"I'm Detective Frank Boscoe of the county sheriff's department. I'm in charge of the investigation into Ruth Wertman's death. If you'd come with me, please, I'd like to ask you some questions about it."

CADE WAITED in the lobby, one eye on what was happening around him, the other on the closed door of Liz Jermain's office. Frank Boscoe and his partner had commandeered it for their questioning, and Talia was still in there with them. As for the rest of what was going on, Liz and the Judge had filled him in on the basics.

While he and Talia had been in the bar, a whole slew of people had arrived from the sheriff's department.

Crime-scene specialists were upstairs now going over room 203 with the proverbial fine-tooth comb. Elsewhere, a team of detectives were questioning people. Two of them had already spoken to him, asking where he'd been at three-forty-five, the time of the murder.

When he told them he'd been in his room and hadn't heard a thing over the sound of the television and the shower, that had been that. But he gathered they were in the process of asking everyone, guests *and* staff, about whether they'd seen or heard anything unusual.

His gaze drifted to where Liz and the Judge had been standing for the past ten minutes—plotting a damage-control strategy, he assumed. By now everyone knew about the murder. And almost all the guests, he'd gathered from bits of conversations, were wondering whether they'd be in any danger if they remained at the resort. He hadn't seen anyone actually check out, but that might only be because the evening ferry had already left.

Finally the Judge turned away from Liz and headed for the stairs. Cade hurried over to intercept him. He had a question that needed an answer.

"Judge Bradshaw?" he called, stopping the older man as he reached the staircase. "Sorry to interrupt you, sir. I know you're busy."

"Oh, I don't mind being interrupted, Cade. I'm just on my way to phone my wife to tell her what's happened, and it's not a conversation I'm looking forward to. In fact, I've been putting off calling her, because I know she's going to be dreadfully upset."

"I can imagine."

The Judge nodded. "She's in Atlanta visiting her brother, and the best thing she could do is just stay put for the moment. But I'm going to have a devil of a time convincing her. You didn't stop me to hear about my wife, though. What can I do for you?"

"I'd just like to ask you something about jury deliberations."

"Oh, I think you should be asking your court officer, not me. I saw Bud going into the dining room, so you could catch him there."

"Well..." Cade thought rapidly. It was going to be pretty obvious why he was asking his question, and the Judge had to be more discreet than Bud. Almost anyone would be. So if he didn't want this talked about, the Judge was his man. "It's nothing to do with our particular jury," he finally tried. "It's just a general question."

"Ah. All right, then, go ahead."

"Well, once a jury's been sequestered, what's the procedure if something happens to one of the jurors?"

"If something *happens* to one of them?"

"Uh-huh." Doing his best to look nonchalant, Cade pressed on. "Say he...has a heart attack or something. Say he ends up in the hospital, and can't take part in the deliberations. Would the others continue on without him, or would there be a new jury selected and a retrial?"

The Judge peered intently at him for a minute. "All right," he finally said, "to give you a *general* answer to your *general* question, if a juror is forced to withdraw, for whatever reason, the remaining eleven jurors would normally continue to deliberate without him. If more than one juror was forced to drop out, the trial judge would decide whether the remaining number should continue or if there should be a retrial."

"I see," Cade said. He had his answer, but it sure wasn't the one he'd wanted.

"Do you think you have just cause to be worried about Talia?" the Judge asked quietly.

Cade met his gaze, wondering exactly how much cause was just under these circumstances. He was sure Joey wouldn't want to go through a retrial, but now he knew that if somebody killed Talia it wouldn't mean a retrial. Was there just cause to worry about that? And there were three jurors convinced Joey was guilty, but if somebody killed Talia there'd be only two. Was there just cause to worry about that?

"I'm not sure, sir," he finally said. "I hope there's not reason to worry, but I'm not sure."

"I hope there's not, too, Cade."

The Judge turned and started up the stairs, leaving Cade with a whole lot of questions he still didn't have answers to. The basic one, of course, hadn't changed. Had Joey sent a one-man welcoming committee to the room Talia was supposed to have checked into? If so, what would happen now?

The killer could still be on the island. Hell, the killer could still be right here hanging around the hotel.

Cade glanced across the lobby, finding that thought damn disturbing.

If the guy was still around, he'd know by now that he'd killed Ruth Wertman, not Talia Sagourin. And the obvious question was, would he try to rectify his mistake?

THE MOLE MADE a point of stopping by Bud the baby-sitter's table and mentioning he was going for an af-ter-dinner walk. Then he headed for the village.

It was only about a mile from the hotel, with the first leg of the road paralleling an open stretch of At-lantic beach. But it wasn't a pleasant walk at this time of night, not with the strong wind gusting in off the ocean.

"Nobody's damn fault you're out here but your own," he muttered to himself. His cell phone wouldn't have run down if he'd remembered to plug it in when they'd arrived at the hotel. And if it hadn't needed charging, his call would've been over and done with by now. He'd be sitting in that nice comfortable bar, in-stead of trudging along out here where it was the fur-thest thing from nice and comfortable.

But he had to find out what the hell was going on, and Joey Carpaccio's goon had been right to warn him about being careful when it came to phones. You never knew who could be listening in at a hotel—especially a hotel where there'd just been a murder.

Mentally reviewing the facts he knew, he decided he really wasn't missing many. Bud was undoubtedly king of the gossip scene no matter where he happened to be.

He'd collected every last detail he could about the killing and been only too happy to share them with any of the jurors who'd cared to listen. But what the mole *didn't* know was whether it should have been Talia Sagourin lying dead, instead of that other woman.

"And room 203 was assigned to our own Talia," Bud had said. "Just think if she'd been the one to walk in there, instead of Ruth Wertman."

Just think. Hell, the mole had scarcely thought about anything else since the moment he'd heard the story. He couldn't stop wondering if killing Talia was that other route the goon had referred to this morning.

He sure as hell hoped it wasn't, because if they killed her it could mean disaster for him. If she ended up dead, the cops would be all over the remaining jurors like fleas on a dog. They'd want to know if anything irregular was going on, and he'd bet they'd find out that there was. And that he was involved in it.

Peering ahead through the darkness, he told himself not to worry so much. He just needed a little reassurance. Not that Joey's goon was exactly the type of guy who instilled confidence, but he was the only potential source of information.

When the mole finally reached the village it was quiet. Most things were closed for the night. He began to wonder if he was out of luck, and then he spotted what he was looking for. Up ahead, outside Ye Olde Sandwich Shop, stood a pay phone. He dug the number from his wallet and took out a credit card, as well—then thought better of using it. Credit transactions could be traced, and he didn't want anyone tracing this.

Fortunately he had a pocketful of change, way more than enough to call Charleston. Now, he thought as the number began to ring, he just needed the goon to be there.

He picked up on the third ring, saying, "Yeah?"

The mole breathed a sigh of relief. "It's me, your friend on Jermain Island."

"Yeah? This phone safe?"

"It's a pay phone. In the middle of nowhere."

"Okay. So what's up?"

"What's up is that some woman got killed here this afternoon. One of the hotel guests. She walked into her room and somebody shot her."

"No bull? I thought it was a classy joint."

"It is. That's not the point."

"So what's the point?"

"The point is, there was a mixup with the rooms. And this woman was murdered in the room Talia Sagourin should've had."

"Yeah?"

"So listen, I need to know, did Mr. Carpaccio have anything to do with it?"

"Why the hell would he wanna kill some woman?"

"Dammit, you know what I mean. Was it supposed to be Talia who got killed?"

"How the hell should I know? Know if it was supposed to be her, I mean. But whoever it was supposed to be, the boss didn't have nothin' to do with it."

"You're sure?"

"Sure I'm sure. You think he's stupid or somethin'?"

"No, of course not. I was just worried, because if someone on this jury gets murdered, the cops will be investigating like crazy. And I sure as hell don't want to end up in jail for helping you out."

"Hey, man, don't get your shorts in a knot, huh? The boss don't want the cops doin' no investigatin', either. So listen, that all you want? 'Cause I'm watchin' basketball here, and the score's tied."

"Yeah . . . yeah, that's all I wanted."

"Well, try not to call me again, huh? You just use that computer of yours. Unless maybe you wanna tell me somethin' real important. Like you got everyone talked into votin' not guilty."

"All right, I'll keep that in mind." The mole hung up, not feeling nearly as happy as he'd like. He had a sense that, in Joey Carpaccio's circle of friends, the right hand didn't always know what the left hand was doing. So maybe the goon didn't know what he was talking about. Or maybe he'd lied.

And if Joey had decided he wanted Talia Sagourin dead . . . well, guys like Joey generally got what they wanted.

Chapter Four

Talia waited while Detective Frank Boscoe sat drumming his fingers on Liz Jermain's desk and staring into space. He was clearly trying to decide whether he and his partner were finished with their inquisition.

She hoped they were. Liz's office, tucked in behind the registration desk, wasn't large. So with the three of them in here and the door closed, it was getting awfully warm.

Finally Boscoe focused on her again. "Well, I think that's all we need for the moment, Ms. Sagourin, although we may want to ask a few more questions later."

"Thank you for your time," Detective Arnie Rebuzo said as she rose and opened the door.

"And I really don't think," Boscoe added, "that you've got anything to worry about. As I said before, the notion you might have been the intended victim is pretty farfetched."

"Yes...I guess it is." She nodded goodbye, then skirted the registration desk, the sight of Cade striding in her direction lifting her spirits a little. For a moment she thought he was going to hug her, and when he didn't she felt a twinge of disappointment. Maybe the lobby wasn't an appropriate place, but she could still have used a hug.

''How'd it go?'' he said by way of a greeting.

''The short version is that they asked questions, I answered them.''

''Well, let's go get some dinner and you can tell me the long version.''

She didn't feel like eating. She *did* feel like some friendly company, though, so she followed Cade into the dining room. It was as elegant as every other part of the hotel she'd seen—tablecloths of crisp white linen, crystal goblets that twinkled in the glow of candlelight and fresh flowers gracing each table. The walls were Wedgwood blue, and she couldn't help thinking Mrs. Wertman would have disapproved. If she'd lived long enough to see them.

When Cade told the maître d' they'd like a quiet table, the man led them to a secluded nook beside the fireplace. Then he flourished menus in front of them and assured them their waiter would be along in a moment.

''So?'' Cade said as the maître d' turned away. ''Let's hear the long version.''

''There's not much to hear. Basically they just had me go over everything that happened from the time I first noticed Mrs. Wertman on the ferry to when Shad and I found her body.''

''And what did they say about your switching rooms with her?''

"They didn't think it was significant." She watched for his reaction to that. She was still worried that it *was* significant, regardless of the detectives' cavalier attitude.

The frown that appeared on Cade's face wasn't at all reassuring. "You told them about wondering if maybe Joey Carpaccio...?"

"Yes. But to quote Frank Boscoe, the idea I might have been the intended victim is pretty farfetched."

"Did he say that *after* you told them that you counsel battered women? That Joey might've found out and decided you'd like to see him fry?"

"Well...I didn't exactly get into that with them."

"What? Why the hell not?"

She shrugged unhappily. "Because the moment I mentioned there was something Joey's lawyers had missed about me during jury selection, they reminded me I could only talk about the trial with other jurors."

"But there must have been some way you could've—"

"Cade, I could tell they didn't think there was the slightest chance that killer was after me. So I was already feeling like a bit of an idiot, which didn't exactly make me eager to—"

"You should've figured out a way to tell them," he interrupted. "Feeling like an idiot isn't the worst thing in the world." He almost pointed out that it wasn't even in the same league as being dead, but managed to stop himself.

"Well, maybe it isn't the worst thing in the world," Talia said, "but they don't think the killer was there intending to shoot anyone. They figure he was a hotel thief who panicked. Which is exactly what Liz and Shad and I concluded in the first place. So. . . I guess the obvious is right."

Cade rubbed his jaw, telling himself that the detectives were the pros here, that they made their living by coming to the right conclusions about things like this. "They don't think there's even a chance the guy was a hired killer?" he finally asked.

"Well . . . not exactly. They admitted it *could* have been a planned hit. But listen to me. I don't even watch cop shows on television, and I sound as if I'm married to the mob. I guess—" she gave a weary smile "—that's what six weeks on a murder-trial jury does to you."

He made himself smile back at her, although they both knew this was no joking matter. After a second he said, "Since they admit it could've been a planned hit, what are they doing on that angle?"

"They've got people looking into things on the mainland. They're checking into what's been happening in Mrs. Wertman's life lately."

"And what about what's been happening in your life lately? What about your being on Carpaccio's jury?"

She shook her head, looking totally frustrated. "Cade, the bottom line is that they said a professional hit man would never have shot Mrs. Wertman by mistake—would never have mistaken her for me, I mean. He'd have had a description of who he was supposed to kill. Probably even a picture. And Mrs. Wertman didn't look anything like me, did she.''

"No...no, nothing like you." Not young and not gorgeous. He tried to force his thoughts from the delectable way Talia looked—even after an hour of playing questions-and-answers with the cops.

"Also," she added, "they pointed out that a planned hit is exactly that—planned in advance."

"Yeah," he muttered. But not all planned hits needed *much* planning.

"And Mrs. Wertman," Talia went on, "made her reservation here weeks ago. Whereas nobody knew I'd be here until after we'd voted this morning."

"And nobody knew Mrs. Wertman was going to hate her room and end up in 203, either. As far as anybody knew, it was your room."

Talia shrugged, although she looked as if she'd rather he hadn't pointed that out. "Cade, all I know is that Boscoe and Rebuzo are sure the murder was a spur-of-the-moment thing. They think Mrs. Wertman just walked in on a thief."

"She walked in on a thief whose gun had a silencer," Cade said.

For a long moment Talia gazed across the table, looking so worried Cade almost wished he'd kept quiet about the silencer.

But he was damn worried himself—worried the good detectives were conveniently ignoring details that didn't fit their spur-of-the-moment theory. They sure wouldn't be the first cops to develop a severe case of tunnel vision.

"We wondered about a thief having a silencer earlier," Talia finally murmured. "Liz and Shad and I. But when I asked Frank Boscoe if it was unusual, he didn't give me a straight answer. You think it is, though, don't you."

Before he could reply their waiter arrived. They hadn't even glanced at the menus, so when he recommended the chef's special, Atlantic salmon in puff pastry, they both ordered it.

"The silencer," Talia said, returning to their topic once the waiter was gone. "It bothered Liz. And if you think there's something strange about it, too..."

He shrugged. "One of my uncles was a cop. And when my brother and I were kids, he used to take us to a shooting range—taught us all about guns. I just can't see a garden-variety hotel thief wandering around with a silencer. Do you know what they look like?"

"No."

"Well, they're metal cylinders that fit over the end of a gun barrel. Fairly long chunky cylinders that make a weapon a whole lot more awkward to carry around. So..." He paused, spotting his channel-surfing roommate.

Harlan was heading across the dining room in their direction, and the big grin on his face was saying Cade just might be one of his favorite people. If that was true, though, the feeling wasn't mutual. Oh, he felt kind of sorry for the guy, but if he'd had his choice of whom to room with, Harlan sure wouldn't have been it.

Cade's glance flickered to Talia, and he fleetingly thought *she* would have been. Then he pushed the thought aside and looked at Harlan once more. The guy was a little taller than average but slightly built, pale and nondescript, with lenses in his glasses as thick as the bottom of a pop bottle. In both appearance and personality, he fit the stereotype of a computer nerd perfectly.

"Cade…Talia," he said, reaching their table. "You guys finished or what?"

"Just ordered," Cade told him.

"Oh…so you won't be coming up to the room with me now, huh?"

"Uh-uh. I'll be along in a while."

Harlan shifted his weight from one foot to the other. "Well, I sure hope when I get up there I don't find a guy waiting for me with a gun." He grinned, but he looked a little anxious. "So," he said after a moment, "I hear you were right there when they found the body, huh, Talia?"

She nodded. "It didn't exactly make my day."

"No…no, I'll bet it didn't. I guess it was pretty gruesome, huh?"

"Yes. Very."

"Was there a lot of blood?"

"Harlan?" Cade said. For a man in his thirties, Harlan was sorely lacking in the social-graces department. "Talia just spent an hour talking to a couple of detectives about the murder, so I think she'd really rather give it a rest now."

"Oh…yeah, I guess she would. So, you guys think we're going to be stuck here more than this one night?"

"I wouldn't be surprised," Talia said. "But you sound as if you hope we're not."

"I do. I don't sleep well in strange places. And I usually look after the motel in the evenings, so it's going to be hard on my mom with me gone day *and* night. She gets nervous, too, if I'm not home at night. So, how long do you think we'll be here?"

"Who knows?" Cade said. "Either until we all agree, or until we decide we'll never reach a unanimous verdict."

"You really think we could end up with a hung jury? When only three people voted guilty? You don't think they'll change their minds? Group pressure and all that stuff?"

"Who knows?" Cade said again.

Harlan looked at Talia. "I guess you were one of the three, huh?"

Before Cade could tell Harlan to mind his own business, Talia said gently, "Why don't we wait till morning to talk about it, Harlan? We're probably better off leaving it until everyone's together."

"Oh. Yeah, I guess. It's just that I'm going up to the room to phone my mom now. And I know she'll ask how many nights I think I'll be away. So I was wondering if you felt real strongly about Joey's being guilty, or if you figure you might change your vote, depending on how everyone else sees things."

"Oh, here's our dinner," Talia said, giving the approaching waiter a relieved smile.

ONCE HARLAN GATES had left, Talia and Cade agreed to concentrate on simply enjoying their food. But even though the salmon was wonderful, Talia couldn't keep her mind off Harlan and his questions.

Why was he so curious about how she'd voted? And about whether or not she might change her mind? Was it really only because he wanted to get home to his mother? She was just about to ask Cade what he thought when the waiter reappeared.

"I was asked to give you this." He handed her a cream-colored envelope with her name written on the front. "And you're both jurors, aren't you?"

When they nodded he said, "Then I won't be bringing you a bill. Everything's looked after. Just let me know if you'd like coffee or anything."

As he turned away Talia pulled the flap open on the unsealed envelope and read the note inside:

My Dear Talia,
I am most distressed that you were involved in the day's unpleasantness and would like to speak privately with you about something related to it.

My wife and I have a suite on the second floor at the far end of the west wing. If you would meet with me there at your earliest convenience, I would be most obliged. As I may have mentioned, my wife is away at present, but I assure you I am a perfect gentleman.

Sincerely,
Judge Cameron Bradshaw.

His final sentence made her smile. The idea of his ever being anything other than a perfect gentleman would never have entered her mind.

She passed Cade the note and watched him read it. "What's wrong?" she asked when his expression grew concerned.

Cade shrugged. "He wants to talk to you because he's worried about you. And if *he* figures there's reason to be worried..."

"What makes you think he's worried?"

"I spoke to him while you were in with the detectives, because it occurred to me we could've been way off base—assuming Joey wanted you dead, I mean. I started thinking that if anything happened to you it might mean a retrial, which I'm sure Joey wouldn't want. So I asked the Judge about it—just in a general way, but he knew why I was asking."

"And what did he say?"

"Well...he said if something happened to one of us, the deliberations would simply proceed with one less juror."

"Oh," she murmured. She'd done her best to convince herself Frank Boscoe and Arnie Rebuzo were right, that the idea Joey had sent someone to kill her was farfetched. But between raising the issue of that silencer and now this, Cade was doing a great job of *un*convincing her, "The Judge still doesn't believe the killer was just a hotel thief," she said uneasily. "Despite what the detectives figure."

"No... that's not necessarily it. He could tell *I* was worried about you, so maybe it was just contagious."

"Like a flu bug."

"Yeah, like a flu bug." Cade gave her a warm smile, but it didn't warm the chill of fear that had settled in her chest.

"And *you're* worried about me," she said at last, "because you still think it could've been me who got killed."

He reached across the table and rested his hand on hers for a moment. "I just don't think," he said quietly, "we should entirely rule out the possibility."

The chill began spreading through her entire body.

"It's nothing more than a possibility, though," he went on. "I'm not saying I'm convinced Joey was behind what happened."

"No... no, of course not." But if everyone except the detectives believed it was even a possibility...

"I'm only saying I think you should be careful. Until the police get the guy. And that's probably what the Judge wants to tell you, too."

"I intend to be careful."

Cade leaned back in his chair, wishing there was some way he could keep an eye on her full-time until they knew exactly what was going on. He *was* worried about her. So damn worried it made him suspect he'd begun caring for her a lot more than he'd realized. A lot more than he'd ever intended.

He sat watching her glance nervously around the dining room, thinking that, as concerned as he was, she had to be a hundred times *more* worried.

When she finally looked back at him she said, "You think the police will get the guy?"

"That's their job." But even if she didn't watch cop shows she had to know there were a lot of killers walking around that the police never caught.

"Where do you think he went afterward?" she asked. "Whoever he was, whatever reason he had for being in that room, did he just jump off the balcony, then coolly walk down to the dock and sit there waiting for the ferry to leave?"

"No, that would've been too risky. If anyone had noticed him waiting, they'd have been able to give the police a description."

"Then what did he do?"

Cade shrugged. "I was thinking he might've come over by private boat and left it docked at the village marina. Bud said the estate owners have things delivered there, remember? And they must have visitors. Which means a strange boat wouldn't draw much attention."

"So he could've just come and gone without anyone realizing. But...there's no guarantee he's actually left, is there."

"Well, no." Ever since that thought had occurred to him, it had been preying on his mind. The killer could easily be hanging around the hotel—the way arsonists often hang around after setting a fire.

"You know, Cade, I once saw a movie about a hotel thief whose MO was to check in as a guest. Then he'd go into the various rooms and steal things. Do you think that might happen in real life?"

"I guess it might."

Talia glanced anxiously around the dining room again. "You don't suppose our murderer could still be right here, do you? Right here in the hotel, I mean?"

"No," he said firmly. But who was to say the guy *wasn't* registered as a guest. And if he had a reason to stay, if he'd made a mistake and killed the wrong woman, for example . . . But hell, they were just going around in circles on this.

Talia sat trying to convince herself the killer was a million miles away. She couldn't manage it, though. For all she knew he was right here in this very room. For all she knew he was watching her this very minute.

She looked at Cade, glad he was with her, glad he was concerned about her, then reluctantly said, "I'd better go up and see the Judge now."

Cade nodded. "I'll help you find his suite." He pulled a couple of bills out of his pocket, tossed them on the table for a tip, and they headed up to the second floor.

"Which is the west wing?" she asked when they reached the top of the stairs.

"This way." He gestured in the opposite direction from their rooms.

"Mr. Hailey?" someone said from behind them.

The someone proved to be a bellboy. "There's an urgent phone call for you, sir. If you'd like to go to your room and dial down to the desk, they'll put it through for you."

Cade glanced at Talia.

"I'll be fine," she assured him. "The Judge's suite?" She asked the bellboy. "Is it along here?"

"Yes, ma'am. Just turn right when you get to the end of this hall and it's down that way."

"Thanks." She looked at Cade once more. "I'll be fine," she told him again.

"Well . . . knock on my door when you're done. Let me know what he had to say."

She nodded, then started away before she lost her nerve. What could possibly happen to her while she was walking down a hallway in an exclusive hotel?

The same thing, an imaginary voice answered, *that happened to Mrs. Wertman when she walked into one of the rooms.*

Trying to ignore the voice, Talia turned right at the end of the hall. Like the rest of the second floor, the west wing hallway stretching ahead of her had antique furniture placed at irregular intervals along it. Big solid pieces that, as she'd thought earlier, would be perfect for a killer to hide behind.

She picked up her pace. Then, a second later, someone pressed something hard into the small of her back and said, "Stop. Don't take another step. And don't turn around. This is a gun."

Chapter Five

Cade turned the key in the lock, giving a quick knock to let Harlan know he was there, but when he opened the door the room was dark and silent.

Switching on the light, he walked over to the phone. He had no idea who'd be calling him here—let alone with any urgency. There shouldn't be problems with the projects his men were working on. Nothing his foreman couldn't handle at least. Checking the number for the desk, he punched it in.

"Front desk," someone picked up.

"There's a call on hold for me," he said. "Cade Hailey, room 227."

"One moment, sir."

He glanced around while he waited, wondering where Harlan had gotten to. He'd said he was coming straight up from the dining room, but there was no sign he'd been here.

"Mr. Hailey?" the voice on the phone said.

"Yes?"

"I'm sorry, sir, but the gentleman who called is no longer on the line."

"He leave a message?"

"No, sir, he didn't."

Cade slowly lowered the receiver, picturing Talia walking toward the Judge's suite alone while he headed in the opposite direction—lured away from her by some unknown caller.

He told himself he'd been reading too many detective novels lately. Then he turned on his heel and started back across the room. Before he reached the door someone knocked, and when he opened it he was standing face-to-face with Frank Boscoe and his partner.

When Boscoe introduced himself, Cade reminded him they'd met earlier in the bar.

"Oh, right," Boscoe said. "Well this," he added, gesturing to his partner, "is Arnie Rebuzo, and we'd like to talk to you for a minute."

Cade stepped back to let them past. Rebuzo closed the door after himself and took a little notebook from his pocket.

"We just want to double-check," Boscoe said, "on something you told one of the other detectives earlier. About where you were at three-forty-five when Mrs. Wertman was murdered."

"I was right here."

"You're sure?" Rebuzo looked at his notebook. "According to the detective you spoke to, you said you walked from the ferry, spent a few minutes in the lobby, then came straight up here to your room. But are you certain you didn't go anywhere else? Or get delayed maybe?"

"I didn't go anywhere else." Cade glanced from one detective to the other. Neither one's expression gave anything away. "And as for getting delayed, I stood in the hall talking to another juror for a few minutes. But Talia said she and Mrs. Wertman came up about ten minutes after I did, so I'd definitely have been in the room by then. Why? What's the problem?"

"The problem is that Harlan Gates says you didn't show up here until almost five," Boscoe said.

"Yeah? Well I don't know why he'd say that, because it's not true. Where do you think I went when I came upstairs if not here?"

"That's what we're trying to establish."

Boscoe's implication was only too clear. But it was also ludicrous, so Cade simply waited to see how far he'd push it.

"Mr. Gates seemed certain of the time," he finally continued. "He said you'd barely walked in before 'Geraldo' came on. And that airs at five."

Cade ran his fingers through his hair, trying to figure out the reason for Harlan's confusion, and then the answer popped into his head. "Oh, I've got it," he said. "There's a simple explanation."

Boscoe looked very interested in hearing it. But before Cade could say another word there was a muted ring and the detective fished a cell phone out of his pocket.

"Excuse me a second," he said, answering it. "He didn't give any details?" he asked after listening briefly. "No? Well, it's probably nothing urgent then, and we've got a couple of other things going. We'll get to his suite as soon as we can."

Boscoe stuck the phone back into his jacket. "Sorry, Mr. Hailey. You were just going to explain about the time discrepancy."

"Right. When the detectives talked to me earlier, they asked if I'd heard Mrs. Wertman scream. And I said I hadn't heard anything, because the TV was on and the shower was running."

Rebuzo checked his notebook, then nodded to Boscoe.

"Well, when I came up to the room," Cade continued, "Harlan was already in the shower. And he was still there when I went out again."

"You went out again," Boscoe repeated.

"Uh-huh. I decided I'd go have a look around the resort. So I guess Harlan just didn't realize I'd been in the room at all."

"I see," Boscoe said, glancing at Rebuzo.

The glance made Cade decidedly uneasy. These guys didn't believe him. They figured he could be their killer.

"And how long were you in the room?" Boscoe asked. "Before you decided to go have your look around?"

"Oh . . . maybe fifteen minutes. My suitcase had already been delivered, so I took time to unpack."

"And Gates was in the shower all that time."

Cade shrugged. "I guess he takes long showers."

Rebuzo wrote something into his notebook, making Cade even more uneasy.

"Mr. Hailey," Boscoe said, "did you know Mrs. Wertman before her death?"

"Of course not. If I had I'd have said so."

"You'd never even heard of her? Never even heard anyone mention her name?"

"Not that I recall," Cade said slowly. One more question, he decided, and he was going to demand a lawyer. Even though that would make these guys *sure* he was guilty.

"Well," Boscoe said, giving him a tight-lipped smile. "I think that's all for now then. Thanks for your help."

Cade trailed them to the door and closed it behind them, not certain who he felt more like killing—Harlan Gates or the good detectives.

"Better keep thoughts like that to yourself, Hailey," he muttered. He'd bet Boscoe and Rebuzo would just love hearing him admit to homicidal impulses.

TALIA HAD BEEN in the Judge's suite for a good twenty minutes, but she was still feeling very shaky. And the Judge didn't seem in much better shape than she was.

She glanced across the coffee table at him again, thinking he looked years older than when they'd first met—even though that had only been this afternoon. It made her wonder if, next time she looked in a mirror, there'd be a middle-aged woman staring back.

"This has certainly been a day we all could have done without," he said.

She nodded. Having a gun stuck in her back was definitely something she could've done without—not to mention the horror of discovering Mrs. Wertman's body. If she ever managed to get to sleep tonight, she'd probably have nightmares on top of her nightmares.

"I just don't understand what happened with that note, Talia. After I told the bellboy to deliver it personally, how did your waiter end up with it?"

She shook her head, but that was one question they'd soon have an answer for. When the Judge had called downstairs and told someone to find Boscoe and Rebuzo, he'd also asked that the bellboy be sent up.

"I should have sealed the envelope," he murmured.

It was at least the tenth time he'd said that, and by this point she could have delivered his next line herself.

"I do hate the taste of the glue on the hotel envelopes, though," he finally added.

"It wasn't your fault," she assured him again. But obviously, the man with the gun had read the note. If he hadn't, how would he have known to lie in wait for her on her way here?

The man with the gun. The man who'd terrified her half to death.

She wished Boscoe and Rebuzo would hurry up and get here, because she wanted to know what they were going to say about the incident. Would it make them admit they'd been wrong earlier? Make them admit that the killer in 203 had probably been waiting for her? That Joey Carpaccio was prepared to do whatever it took to keep from ending up on death row?

That *whatever* included having a juror killed so she wouldn't be able to vote guilty?

"Would you like coffee or anything?" The Judge asked, bringing her back to the moment.

"No, thanks. I'm fine."

Liar, an imaginary voice accused. And it was right. She certainly wasn't fine. The scene in the hallway was persistently replaying in her head. And each time it did, she felt terrified all over again.

"Stop," the man had said, his voice a hoarse whisper. "Don't take another step. And don't turn around. This is a gun."

She could still feel its hardness against her back, could still hear the man's sinister tone.

"I just want you to know how vulnerable you are," he'd continued. "You understand how easy it would be to take you out?"

When she'd nodded, her knees weak with fear, he'd told her to count to a hundred before she moved a muscle. And by the time she'd done that he was long gone. Her heart had been pounding so loudly she hadn't even heard the sound of his footsteps as he'd left.

Before the scene could begin replaying yet again, the bellboy arrived, and the Judge ushered him into the living room.

"Don't be nervous, son," he said. "I just want to ask you about the note I gave you for Ms. Sagourin, here. She says you didn't deliver it personally, that her waiter brought it to her."

The boy anxiously glanced at her, then back at the Judge. "I know you told me to give it right to her, sir. But when I got to the dining room the maître d' stopped me. He said he didn't want me tracking through, so he'd see that she got it."

"Ah. I assumed it must have been something like that."

"I . . . I didn't think I should argue with him, sir."

"No. You were right not to. So, you took it straight downstairs and left it with the maître d', is that correct? No detours on the way? It never left your hands until you got to the dining room?"

"No, sir."

"Fine, that's all I wanted to know. Thank you for coming up."

"No problem, sir. So . . . should I just get back to work now, or what?"

"Yes. Yes, you do that. I imagine the police will want to talk to you in due course, but don't start worrying about it."

"No, sir," he murmured. His expression when he left, though, told Talia he was already worrying about it.

"Well," the Judge said, "I believe I'll just call the dining room and have the maître d' and your waiter come up. I doubt Detective Boscoe is going to appreciate our doing his work for him, but I'm too old to worry about things like that. And I'm sure you'd like nothing better than to get to the bottom of this."

She tried to smile, but it didn't feel right. What she'd really like better than anything else was to be certain she'd be getting off this island alive.

DETECTIVE FRANK BOSCOE, partner Arnie Rebuzo in tow, got to the Judge's suite before the maître d' and the waiter. Not long before, but long enough for Talia to walk them through her encounter in the hall.

Just as she was finishing, the other two men arrived, and Boscoe asked the maître d' to tell him exactly what had happened to the note after he'd taken it from the bellboy.

"Well," he said, his glance darting to the Judge, "just as I took it, a couple arrived to be seated. So I put the envelope down on top of the reservations book for a second."

"And the reservations book is where?" Boscoe asked.

"Right at the entrance to the restaurant."

"Okay, so you put it down for a second. And then?"

"I took the couple to their table."

"Leaving the envelope where it was."

The maître d' nodded.

"And the front of it? With Ms. Sagourin's name written on it? Was that facing up or down?"

"I...I'm not sure, but it was probably up, because I'd just looked at it."

"All right. So you took this couple to their table. Then did you return to the entrance right away?"

"No, not exactly right away. The gentleman wanted to know if we had any special wines in the cellar that weren't on the wine list. So I told him about those. Then they talked a little about a wine-tasting tour they'd just been on in France."

"So all this actually took a lot longer than a second," Boscoe said. "How much longer, would you say?"

The maître d' shot another glance in the Judge's direction, then looked at Boscoe again. "Maybe ten minutes? But the second I got back to the entrance, I gave the note to Rod," he added, nodding toward the waiter.

"And you," Boscoe said, turning his attention to the younger man, "took it directly to Ms. Sagourin?"

"Yes. Immediately."

"But in the meantime," Boscoe said, "it was sitting where anyone going in or out of the restaurant—or even just walking by the entrance—could have had a look at it."

"Well . . . yes," the maître d' admitted.

Boscoe nodded. "That's all for the moment then, gentlemen. We'll let you get back to the dining room."

The moment the Judge closed the door behind them, Talia turned to Boscoe. "The man in the hall was Mrs. Wertman's killer, wasn't he."

"What makes you say that?"

She glared at him. She was lucky to still be alive, and there was no guarantee she'd stay that way. So she wanted answers, not more of his stupid questions.

"Well, let's see," she said, trying not to sound totally sarcastic. "Mrs. Wertman was killed with a gun in the room *I* was supposed to have. And now I've had a gun stuck in my back and been warned how easy it would be to take me out. Does anything add up there?"

"I doubt it," Boscoe said.

"What? How can you say that with a straight face? Somebody wants me dead! And I know I'm not supposed to say a word to anyone about the trial, or about whether I think the accused is guilty, or name any names, but you know exactly who I mean!"

"Ms. Sagourin, try to calm down," Arnie Rebuzo told her. "Now, I don't know if what I'm going to say will make you feel better or worse, but if somebody really wanted you dead, odds are you wouldn't be standing here yelling at us."

"I am not yelling!"

"The point my partner's making," Boscoe put in, "the point I was trying to make, is that things don't add up. Not the way you're adding them up at least. You're saying someone killed Mrs. Wertman because he thought she was you. But now that he's got your identity straightened out, he merely walks up behind you and frightens you?"

"Going from murdering to threatening," Rebuzo said, "is the wrong way around. First you get threatened, *then* you get killed. Nobody starts off shooting and de-escalates to a threat."

"Exactly." Boscoe took over again. "And the threat itself doesn't make sense, either. Real threats are specific, not vague like his. Why tell you that you'd be easy to kill, but not why he'd want to? Or what he wanted you to do so he wouldn't? I'm not sure what's going on here yet, but I think that guy in the hall might just have been some weirdo. If he really wanted you dead, he would've killed you right there when he had the chance.''

CADE LOOKED UP from his book, not sure if he'd heard a sound from the next room or only imagined it. But either Talia had changed her mind about stopping by to let him know what the Judge had wanted, or she'd been talking to the old fellow for a heck of a long time.

Telling himself the Judge was probably lonely with his wife away, Cade went back to his novel. A minute later his eyes strayed to the door that connected 227 and 225. If Talia was in there he wanted to see her. Maybe the Judge had gotten her even more upset. Or maybe...

Well, regardless of how many possible reasons he came up with, the bottom line was that he wanted to see her. And even though the door was locked on both sides, there was nothing to stop him from giving a tap to see if she was there.

While he was still considering the idea, someone knocked from the hall. He pushed himself out of the chair and headed for the door, hoping it wasn't Boscoe and Rebuzo. If the good detectives paid him another visit they'd probably come armed with an arrest warrant.

When he opened the door and saw Talia, he smiled. She didn't smile back. She just stood there, looking as frightened as a trapped rabbit. Even though it made him want to put his arms around her and assure her she was safe, he didn't. He figured, if he was really careful, there was still a chance he could win his game of look-but-don't-touch. He'd begun to doubt it was a very good chance, though. And ever since he'd discovered that the thought of something happening to her made him go ice cold inside, he'd been wondering if he shouldn't just give up on his game altogether.

He gestured her into the room, but she didn't move. She simply whispered, "Is Harlan in there?"

"No. What's wrong?"

She glanced along the hallway, then at him again. "Would you mind coming to my room? I don't want him arriving and interrupting us."

"Sure." He stepped out into the hall and closed the door, wondering what the hell the Judge had said to shake her up so badly. The minute they were inside her room, he asked.

"Oh, Cade," she answered, "it wasn't anything Judge Bradshaw said. You were right—he only wanted to talk to me because he was worried about me. He just wanted to be sure I'd be careful. But before I got there... when I was halfway down that hall, someone stuck a gun in my back."

Cade stared at her, his throat dry and the ice-cold feeling back again. Then he remembered the phone call that had made him leave her on her own, and the feeling changed to one of horror. He hadn't just been reading too many detective novels, after all. Someone *had* wanted to lure him away from her. But since she already looked so damn frightened, he decided not to tell her that at the moment.

"Are you all right?" he said, instead. "He didn't actually harm you?" When she shook her head, he began to breathe a little more easily. "Good. That's the main thing. So what happened after he stuck the gun in your back?"

Talia shrugged, looking so close to tears that Cade gave up all hope of being able to keep his distance.

"Hey," he said, putting his arms around her. "You're okay. And you're safe now."

As he pulled her close, her scent wafted enticingly over him. Evocative of sea air and cool sand, it never failed to make him think of a secluded stretch of beach in the moonlight. And when she pressed her cheek against his chest he could feel his heart beginning to beat faster. She was as soft and warm in his arms as he'd known she'd be. So soft and warm he found himself hoping that if time ever stood still she'd be in his arms when it happened.

"Just relax," he whispered into her hair. "Just relax and tell me when you can."

"He said," she finally murmured, "that he wanted me to know how vulnerable I am. How easy it would be to kill me."

Cade swore silently and hugged her a little more tightly. He wasn't going to let anyone kill her. Whatever the hell was going on, he'd see that nothing more serious happened to her than already had.

"I assume," he said after a minute, "the guy's voice didn't sound familiar?"

"No. It was muffled. Just a hoarse whisper. I'm sure it was a man, but that's all." As she finished speaking Talia drew away a little.

Reluctantly Cade let his arms fall to his sides. He'd known what would happen if he relaxed his don't-touch rule, and sure enough it had. She'd felt so good that now he wanted to kiss her—even though he knew this was one hell of a time to start getting romantic.

"What about the cops?" he asked, shoving his hands into his pockets so he couldn't reach for her again. "Have you talked to them yet?"

She nodded. "The Judge called Boscoe. So I've just had another session with him and Rebuzo."

"And?"

The wan smile she gave Cade made him want to kiss her even more. "And basically," she said, "they admitted they don't know what's going on."

Cade simply shook his head. The fact that the good detectives didn't know what was going on was hardly a news flash. They obviously figured the killer could be almost anyone. That was the only explanation for them having questioned *him* a second time.

But if the killer could be almost anyone, then hell, he could also be almost *anywhere*.

That thought drove the lingering temptation to kiss Talia completely out of Cade's mind. "Look," he said, glancing toward the balcony. "I want you to tell me all the details of what they said. But I'd feel better if I had a quick look around first, okay?"

Chapter Six

Cade didn't bother waiting for Talia's answer. He simply walked over to the bathroom and made sure no surprise visitor was lurking there. After checking the closets he headed out through the French doors.

The night was starry and moonlit, no black shadows to conceal anyone. And since the walls separating the balconies were only waist high, he could see that the adjoining ones were empty, as well.

Reassured, he went back inside and sat down on the love seat beside Talia. "So, fill me in on exactly what Boscoe and Rebuzo said this time around."

"First let me tell you how the guy knew I'd be going to the Judge's suite."

She proceeded to tell him about how the Judge's note had been left lying around, how practically anybody could have read it. From there, she moved on to what had happened with Boscoe and Rebuzo. But she'd barely gotten started on that before Cade could see she was close to crying, her blue eyes growing wet with tears.

Before they spilled over he suggested she take a break from the story. When she nodded, he put his arm around her shoulders, then simply sat stroking her golden hair and breathing in that beach-in-the-moonlight scent.

It was dangerously bewitching. And her body against his was even more bewitching...even more dangerous. But he could no more run for the hills under these circumstances than he could have during the trial, when he'd first become aware of the effect she had on him.

And hell, foolish as it probably was, he no longer had the slightest desire to run. Not for the moment, anyway. All he wanted to do while they were stuck on this island was ensure that nothing more happened to her.

Finally she leaned back against the couch and looked at him. "You know what I think bothers me most?"

He shook his head.

"Well, besides being scared half to death, it's that I can't make any sense of all this. Until I talked to Boscoe and Rebuzo, things at least seemed to add up. I was back to the theory that Joey Carpaccio's hit man had mistaken Mrs. Wertman for me. Then when he discovered he'd made a mistake, he pulled his stunt in the hall."

Cade waited. It sounded straightforward to him.

"But it *doesn't* add up," Talia continued. "Boscoe put it perfectly. He said if the guy in the hall had really wanted me dead, he'd have killed me right then and there.''

''Well—'' Cade hesitated ''—maybe he didn't because the place is swarming with cops now. That doesn't make it the best time to kill someone. Or maybe he figured he could scare you enough to make you vote the right way.''

''Then why didn't he tell me that's what he wanted? It's because he didn't say a word about the deliberations that Boscoe and Rebuzo don't think he has anything to do with Joey Carpaccio. In fact, Rebuzo practically came right out and said that if Carpaccio had told someone to kill me, I'd already be dead.''

''Well, if they don't think he had anything to do with Joey, what the hell *do* they think? I mean, I know you said they don't have a clue, but surely they have some ideas.''

Talia shrugged wearily. ''Their best guess is that he's just some weirdo. Either a hotel guest or somebody on staff. By now everyone knows the whole story and knows I've got to be a bundle of nerves. So maybe he *was* just somebody getting his jollies at my expense.''

''Dammit, Talia, that doesn't sound like much of a best guess to me. I think Boscoe and Rebuzo are just grasping at straws. And not only about your guy in the hall. Do you know why you waited so long for them to get to the Judge's suite?

''Partly,'' he went on when she shook her head, ''because when they got the call saying that the Judge wanted to see them, they were busy in my room— practically accusing me of Mrs. Wertman's murder.''

"No," she said, shaking her head again.

"I'm serious. I was starting to worry about how soon I'd find myself in a courtroom again. And I don't mean as a juror."

Talia managed a smile, but it was such an incredibly fleeting one it tugged at his heart.

"I just don't know," she murmured. "Maybe they *are* only grasping at straws. But it *could* have been a weirdo. There are a lot of people walking around loose who shouldn't be. I see examples of it all the time in my practice." She paused, shaking her head. "It's just so damn spooky, because he knew who I was and intercepted that note and . . . it was all so organized."

Cade cleared his throat uneasily. The time had come to fill her in on exactly *how* organized. She had to have all the facts, even though telling her was going to make her even more frightened. "That message," he forced himself to begin, "the one I got when I was walking you to the Judge's suite? Saying there was a phone call for me?"

She nodded.

"When I got to my room and called downstairs about it the guy had hung up. And even though it was supposedly urgent, he hadn't left a message. And he didn't phone back."

For a moment Talia just gazed at him blankly. Then those gorgeous eyes of hers grew wide with fresh fear.

"Oh, Lord," she murmured. "Of course. He had to have been right there in the dining room to have read that note. So he knew you were with me."

"And he wanted you alone," Cade said quietly.

Talia simply sat staring across the room for a minute, then looked at him again. "Cade? Why on earth would Boscoe and Rebuzo think *you* might have murdered Mrs. Wertman?"

He shrugged. "I can't prove where I was when she was killed."

"But I thought you were in your room with Harlan."

"I was, but Harlan didn't see me. That hadn't occurred to me until the detectives asked about it. But when I first came upstairs, Harlan was in the shower. And I went out to have a look around before he was done."

"So he was in the shower when Mrs. Wertman was murdered?"

"Right."

"But if he didn't see you, then you didn't see him, either."

"No, of course not."

"Then how," Talia said slowly, "do you know he really *was* in the shower? How do you know he didn't just leave the water running and go out?"

IT ALL ADDED UP to Harlan Gates. Talia glanced at Cade, sitting on the love seat opposite hers, and tried to remember which of them had been first to realize that.

She wasn't sure, but that was why they'd moved from her room to Cade and Harlan's, deciding that when Harlan showed they'd see what he had to say for himself. Oh, they didn't actually believe he'd snuck out of his room—shower running—and murdered Mrs. Wertman. Once they'd talked about that, they'd decided it was a pretty absurd idea.

In the first place, even though Harlan was a little strange, neither of them could really believe he was a homicidal maniac. And in the second place, he'd known Cade would be getting to their room any minute. So if he hadn't been showering, and Cade had been there when he'd come back to the room . . . well, it was just too absurd.

But the possibility Harlan had been the guy in the hall didn't seem the least bit unbelievable, because the more they'd talked about Frank Boscoe's weirdo theory the more sense they'd decided it made.

She shook her head, imagining what her professional colleagues would think about something called a weirdo theory. It was hardly a term the American Psychological Association would sanction. But setting that quibble aside, it made sense that nobody would go from murder to a threat of murder. Which made it unlikely the guy in the hall had been one of Joey Carpaccio's friends.

That left them with the weirdo theory. And Harlan Gates was both their closest certifiable weirdo and the most obvious suspect. He'd been in the dining room, so he'd have walked straight past the Judge's note. He could easily have read it. Then, all he'd had to do was hang around until he'd seen they were finished eating. Once they were, Harlan could have called the desk from a pay phone to get Cade waylaid, then gone upstairs to lie in wait for Talia.

Of course, he'd have needed a motive, as well as the opportunity, and that was the weak link. There was no obvious motive. But even though people tended to keep their deepest secrets hidden, she suspected Harlan's relationships with women weren't particularly healthy. And if he leaned toward the sadistic, he'd have thoroughly enjoyed scaring the hell out of her.

She looked at Cade again, wishing Liz Jermain had put him in a room with one of the other jurors. *Any* of the others.

"Where the hell's Harlan?" Cade muttered, glancing over and catching her gaze.

The warm concern in his gray eyes made her wish she was sitting right beside him, the way they'd been in her room. Then he could easily put his arms around her and hold her again. Merely thinking about her body pressed against his was enough to start a fluttering around her heart, and being close to him had made her feel comforted and protected. And far more than that.

She'd wanted to kiss him so much she'd barely been able to stop herself. One minute she'd been scared half to death. The next she'd been in Cade's arms and aware only of his lips mere inches from hers. But even though she'd always thought of herself as a liberated woman, some primitive inner voice—undoubtedly imprinted by her mother and grandmother and a hundred earlier female ancestors—had told her to wait for him to make the first move.

He hadn't made it, though. And when he hadn't she'd almost been reduced to tears right there in his arms. But now that she had her emotions under control and was thinking sensibly once more, she knew it had been just as well.

Until she'd completely sorted out what was going on, until she was sure there wasn't somebody intending to scare the devil out of her again—or worse—she had to keep her wits about her. And she'd bet her life that kissing Cade Hailey would render her totally witless.

She'd bet her life. Bad phrase, she told herself, looking at him again.

"I still don't think we should waste our time talking to Harlan," he muttered. "I still think I should just break his neck the minute he walks through that door." His expression said he was only half joking. "You're sure that's a bad idea?" he added when Talia shook her head.

"Positive. We aren't a hundred percent certain it was him."

"I'm a hundred percent certain."

"Well, it's still a bad idea. If you break his neck you'll get arrested for murder."

"Then can I at least push him off the balcony? The most that would break is an arm or a leg."

Talia smiled—with surprisingly little effort. The situation no longer seemed half as grim. They'd talk to Harlan, and things would probably be all right once he knew they were on to him.

Then she glanced toward the bed Cade had told her was Harlan's and felt a little less sure that talking to him would take care of the problem. He'd left the TV remote on his bedside table, lined up perfectly parallel to the edge. And on the dresser, his laptop and printer were precisely centered—as if he'd carefully measured in all directions before setting them down.

Not that obsessive behavior always indicated serious pathology. Sometimes, though...

Finally deciding she'd worried in silence long enough, she said, "Cade?"

"Uh-huh?"

"Maybe you should tell Bud you want to room with someone else. I'm sure he'd get somebody to switch with you."

"Switch with me and get stuck with Harlan? Nobody'd be very happy about that idea, especially not now that they're settled in. Besides, maybe it's just as well I'm with him. This way, I can keep an eye on him."

Good point, she thought. She'd feel a whole lot better knowing someone she trusted was keeping an eye on their weirdo. And she really was convinced Harlan wasn't a homicidal maniac, so it was awfully unlikely that Cade's safety was at risk.

If she actually believed Harlan was dangerous, they wouldn't be sitting here waiting to confront him. Instead, she'd have insisted on letting Boscoe and Rebuzo handle the situation—despite Cade's feeling that the detectives wouldn't take their suspicions seriously. He was sure they'd figure it was just a ploy to cause Harlan grief. To get back at him for saying Cade hadn't been in their room when Mrs. Wertman was killed.

At any rate, she was certain they could handle Harlan on their own. He was simply a man with a warped psyche, and warped psyches were her specialty.

"Show time," Cade suddenly whispered.

At the same instant she heard a key in the lock. Her pulse leapt. Cade, though, leaned back in his seat, looking the picture of composure.

The door swung open and Harlan paused in the doorway, obviously surprised to find Talia in his room. "Hey, Cade...Talia."

His speech, she thought, seemed slightly slurred. And when he closed the door and started across the room he didn't look too steady on his feet.

"Where've you been?" Cade asked.

Harlan flopped onto the edge of his bed and began taking off his shoes before answering. "Some of the guys were in the bar, so I had a couple of beers with them." He reached over and grabbed the remote. "You two mind if I watch a little TV?"

"Actually," Cade said before he switched it on, "we want to ask you about something."

"Yeah?" Harlan shot them a puzzled look.

"Yeah. Earlier, when we were talking to you in the dining room, you said you were on your way up to the room. To phone your mother."

"Yeah."

"But you didn't come up here."

"Sure I did."

Cade shook his head. "I was here, Harlan. Not long afterward. And you hadn't been here, had you?"

"Oh...well, actually, no."

"So where were you?"

"What's it to you?"

"Harlan," Talia said quietly, "somebody stuck a gun in my back and threatened me."

Harlan eyed her uncertainly. "You aren't saying you think it was me...are you?"

"We're just asking where you were," Talia said.

Harlan wiped his hand across the back of his mouth, not taking his eyes off her. "Hey," he said at last, "you guys joking around or what?"

"No joke," Cade said.

Harlan glanced at him, then back at Talia. "Look, the only gun I own is behind the desk at the Gates Motel. I left it there for my mom. But even if I had it here, why would I want to threaten you?"

"I don't know. Would you?"

"Good God, Talia," he snapped. "Who do you think you are? Ace Ventura?"

"Just tell us where you went after you left the dining room," Cade demanded. "You said you were coming up to the room, but you didn't. So what did you do? That's all we're asking."

"This is really making me mad, you know!"

Talia caught Cade's eye and pressed her lips together, telling him to try letting the silence work for them. He gave her an almost imperceptible nod and they simply waited.

Eventually Harlan focused on Cade and said, "I didn't come upstairs because I didn't want to have to walk in here by myself. Okay? You were still sitting in the dining room and ... Look, I know it sounds stupid, but who's to say the killer won't strike again? So I phoned my mom from downstairs. Then I just wandered around for a while and finally went to the bar, hoping some of the other guys would be there. That satisfy you?"

CADE WALKED TALIA next door in silence, then did his bathroom and balcony check once more—carefully locking the French doors when he came back in. He knew he was only making her more nervous, but he had to be certain she was safe before he left.

"What do you think?" she asked when he was done. "You still think it was Harlan?"

"I don't know. What about you?"

She shrugged. "I don't know, either. But if it wasn't him, who on earth was it?"

Cade merely shook his head. There wasn't much point in saying he didn't know again. He seemed to be saying it every second sentence.

"If anything bothers you during the night," he told her, instead, "anything at all, remember I'm just on the other side of that connecting door."

"So's Harlan," she murmured.

"Yeah, well..." Cade gazed at her and tried to make himself start back to his own room.

The longer he stayed here the greater the risk he was going to do something really stupid. But she looked so desperately in need of a hug that he could feel his willpower disappearing like smoke on a windy day.

"Look," he said at last, "if you're going to be afraid in here on your own I could stay. I'm sure we could get a cot brought in or something."

For a minute he thought she was going to say yes, and it almost made him wish he hadn't opened his mouth. She had to be incredibly vulnerable at the moment. So the only right thing to do was play the perfect gentlemen. But he was a normal, red-blooded male. And if he ended up spending all night in here with her...

Then she murmured, "No," and he wished she'd said "Yes."

She said, "No" a second time, almost as if she had to convince herself it was the right decision, then added, "I'd just as soon not be the subject of rumors and innuendos tomorrow. And if you spent the night in my room I'll bet Harlan would be only too happy to tell everyone about it."

"Well, I guess I'll get going then." He resisted with all his might, but the words still came out. "Unless you think a hug might make you feel better."

"Oh, Cade, I think it would make me feel a whole lot better."

When she moved closer, he wrapped his arms around her and simply held her, breathing in her intoxicating scent once more. Then, resting his chin on her head, he closed his eyes and told himself he was a fool. The way she made him feel . . .

Silently he cursed himself for letting this happen. Maybe someday he'd find another woman he could risk falling in love with, but he should have been more careful around Talia. He'd known all along that spending so much time with her was playing with fire, and he'd already been burned badly enough to last a lifetime.

Since he hadn't been more careful, though, all he could do now was try to ignore the fact he'd become addicted to her scent. Ignore the rush he felt when she walked into the room. Ignore the way he was feeling this very moment, with her body soft and warm and lush against his. He wanted to kiss her so much he could taste it.

But if he kissed her he'd be done for. He'd never be able to stop at a kiss or two. And what kind of guy would take advantage of a woman in the shape she was in? A woman who probably wasn't even thinking straight?

No, this definitely wasn't the time or place—regardless of how he was feeling.

He held her for a few more seconds, until she looked up and murmured, ''Thanks, Cade. A hug was exactly what I needed.''

''Glad I could help out,'' he managed hoarsely, relieved that his voice was still working at all. The warmth of her breath on his neck had almost done him in.

"Well, see you in the morning," she whispered when he dropped his arms and stepped away.

Once he made it to the door that separated their rooms, he risked looking back. "Don't forget to lock this behind me. And don't forget how close I am."

"I won't." She gave him a little smile that warmed his heart.

He forced himself to step into his own room, knowing *he* sure as hell wouldn't be forgetting that they were so close. He'd probably lie awake all night, thinking about nothing except her in her bed, just on the other side of that damn connecting door.

Chapter Seven

By the time Cade heard the lock click on Talia's side of the door he was wondering whether she slept nude, as he did, or if he should be imagining her in a sexy nightgown. Then David Letterman's voice brought his musings to an abrupt end.

Dave was in the midst of working his way through one of his Top Ten lists, but Harlan seemed oblivious to that. He was sitting on his bed, propped up against the headboard, furiously keyboarding on his laptop. He'd changed into a pair of black kung fu pajamas, which made Cade realize he hadn't thought to bring anything to sleep in. It had been a long time since he'd shared a room with anyone.

When Harlan didn't even look up from his computer, let alone say anything, Cade simply walked past the beds and into the bathroom. For all he cared, Harlan could stay angry at him the entire time they were stuck here. Hopefully that wouldn't be for long.

He grabbed his bathrobe from the bathroom door, thankful he'd at least remembered to bring it, and decided he'd better sleep in his briefs. After he'd finished in the bathroom he marched past Harlan's bed again, climbed into his own, and turned his back to the glow from the bedside lamp.

On the television, Letterman had progressed to a segment of Stupid Pet Tricks, and Cade was certain Harlan had upped the volume just to annoy him. For a few minutes he lay listening to Dave's wisecracks, the laughter of his studio audience, the wailing of a dog imitating a country-and-western singer, and the clicking of Harlan's keyboard. Then his patience gave out.

He sat up and glared at his roommate. "Look," he said, "we're supposed to start deliberating at nine-thirty in the morning. So do you think you could knock it off for the night?"

"What I think," Harlan said, finally looking at him, "is that you owe me an apology. Talia, too. But I'll settle for just yours at the moment."

Cade thought about that for a minute and realized that if Harlan really *wasn't* their weirdo, he was right. They did owe him apologies.

"All right," he said. "If we jumped to the wrong conclusions, I'm sorry."

"Fine." Harlan clicked Letterman into oblivion. As the TV went dark, he turned off his laptop, closed it and carried it to the dresser.

"My mom," he announced, heading back across the room, "always says people should never go to bed mad."

That said, he got into bed and switched off the light, leaving Cade with the unsettled feeling that Harlan had just behaved more maturely than he had.

He punched his pillow a few times, then tried to go to sleep. But just as he'd expected, sleep wouldn't come. He simply lay there thinking about Talia, about how damn good it had felt to hold her. He let himself dwell on that for a few minutes, then couldn't keep his thoughts from moving on to what it would be like to kiss her... touch her... make love to her.

Forcing his thoughts from that, he started working his way through every trick he knew to help himself fall asleep, until he made it into that never-never land where you slipped back and forth between sleep and waking.

He drifted there for a while. And then he shot bolt upright, a scream ringing in his ears.

For a second he thought he'd been dreaming. Then there was another scream and he knew it was for real. And, oh, God, it had come from Talia's room.

Frantically he fumbled in the darkness, trying to locate the switch on the bedside lamp. Finally he found it and light spilled onto his bed—and over Harlan's empty one.

TALIA SCREAMED in terror once more. The man still didn't move. He stood motionless on her balcony, a black shape illuminated by the moonlight.

The sheers prevented her from seeing him clearly, but she could make out that he had his arms raised and his palms pressed against two of the panes in the French doors. When she tried to get out of bed she discovered her legs were frozen with fear. Frozen, yet trembling at the same time. Her entire body was trembling. She was going to die in this bed, the victim of some psychotic killer.

The door was locked, but all he had to do was break one of those panes of glass and—

"Talia!"

At first she didn't know who was shouting her name. Then she realized it was Cade, that he was pounding on the door between their rooms.

"Talia!" he yelled again. "Unlock the door!"

His words spurred her into action. She flew out of bed and across the dark room, her heart racing. When she couldn't get the door unlocked, tears began streaming down her face. Then the lock clicked, the door opened, and she was in Cade's arms.

"What happened?" he whispered against her hair.

An instant later she felt his body tense.

"Oh, my God," he said. He grabbed her firmly by the shoulders, pushed her against the wall and started across the room.

It wasn't until he reached a moonlit patch in the darkness that she noticed he was wearing only a pair of white briefs. It made him seem so vulnerable to harm that fresh fear flooded her—fear for him this time. She tried to call his name, tried to tell him not to go near the balcony, but no sound came out.

He paused to grab something that was glinting silver on the dresser, something a stray moonbeam had caught. Then he continued on, clutching the object like a knife. Talia stared at it, finally realizing he'd grabbed her comb. He was going to confront a crazed killer with only her steel rat-tail comb for a weapon.

When it dawned on her she should be doing something to help she started for the phone. But before she reached it Cade shouted, "Harlan! What the hell are you doing out there?"

She turned and stared through the darkness at the moonlit balcony. Cade was standing in front of the French doors now, close enough to have identified Harlan through the sheers.

"Harlan!" he yelled again. "Harlan, what the hell's the matter with you?"

Something clicked in her head. "Wait," she said. "Don't say anything more. Let me come over there and have a look at him."

Cade shoved the sheers aside and she could see Harlan clearly now. He didn't move as she walked toward the balcony doors. His palms were still pressed against two panes of glass, and he was staring straight at her, but she doubted he saw a thing.

"He's sleepwalking," she murmured.

"What?"

"I think he's sleepwalking."

"Well, I think he's faking! I—"

"Cade, let me handle this, okay?"

The look he shot her said he didn't like that idea one bit. And even though he didn't try to stop her when she unlocked the doors, he was brandishing the pointed end of her comb like a stiletto.

"Harlan?" she said quietly, opening the doors and resting her hand on his arm. "Harlan, you'd better come inside. It's cold out there."

She drew him into the room. "We're just going to walk you back to bed now," she told him.

"Talia," Cade whispered, "are you sure you know what you're doing?"

"Yes," she assured him even though she wasn't. She'd certainly studied a little about somnambulism, even recalled watching a video on it. But she'd never actually seen anyone sleepwalking, let alone dealt with it.

But was sleepwalking what Harlan was doing? Or was he faking, as Cade had suggested?

"Come on, Harlan," she murmured, starting off, her hand still on his arm. He willingly walked across the room with her. Cade followed on their heels, his skepticism so strong the air was thick with it.

She led Harlan through the connecting door, and he happily crawled into bed and curled up under the blankets. When he closed his eyes she glanced at Cade. He was staring at Harlan and didn't notice her looking, so she let her eyes linger.

The light from the bedside lamp was playing over his near-naked body, painting planes and hollows in all the right places. And undressed, he was even more attractive than he was dressed. Broad shoulders, a flat stomach and lean muscles everywhere they should be. It made her wonder if he worked out, in addition to the physical labor he did on his company's projects.

Then he unexpectedly looked at her, and she felt her face flush. Not only had he caught her watching him, but now he was staring at her exactly the same way she'd been staring at him. And it was hardly surprising. She wasn't exactly fully dressed herself. She tugged on the bottom of her nightshirt, but that only made the silk cling more tightly to her breasts.

Cade finally looked away, grabbing a bathrobe off the floor beside his bed and saying, "Shouldn't we wake him up? Find out what the hell the deal is?"

"No. It's hard to wake a sleepwalker. And he wouldn't remember what happened, anyway."

"He would if he's *not* a sleepwalker," Cade whispered. He shoved his arms into the sleeves of his robe, then nodded toward the still-open door between their rooms. "Let's go. I want to get away from Sleeping Beauty and talk to you."

He hustled her back into her own room and closed the door, saying, "I don't like this. Never mind just being a weirdo, Harlan's as crazy as a loon."

"Cade, the man was sleepwalking."

"You're sure about that?"

"Well . . . yes," she murmured, easing her way over to where *her* robe was lying.

"You don't sound very sure to me."

"Well, I'm pretty sure." She shrugged into the robe and tied it tightly around her. "If he wasn't he knows exactly what a sleepwalker looks like. Plus, he's an awfully good actor."

Cade eyed her dubiously.

"It's not that rare a disorder. It also doesn't mean he's crazy."

"No? Well what if he *is* just an awfully good actor? And what if he was the guy in the hall tonight? If he was, then he was trying to get in here so he could scare the blazes out of you again. Or...or who the hell knows what he had in mind this time?''

Talia tried to think. There was no denying Cade might be right. She had no way of knowing if Harlan was actually a sleepwalker or not. Unless...

"I'm going to phone his mother," she said.

"What?"

"I'm going to get the number from information, then I'm going to phone his mother."

Cade glanced at her bedside clock. "Talia, it's after two in the morning."

"Which means I'll frighten her half to death and she'll hate me for not having waited until morning. But we've got to know the truth. At least *I've* got to know it. And I want to talk to her before Harlan has a chance to."

THE WOMAN WHO ANSWERED the phone sounded both anxious and groggy.

"Mrs. Gates?" Talia said.

"Yes?"

She nodded to Cade, who was sitting on the other love seat watching her. "Mrs. Gates, my name is Talia Sagourin. I feel dreadful about waking you in the middle of the night, but I'm on the Carpaccio jury with Harlan. I'm calling from the Bride's Bay Resort."

"Oh, no," she whispered. "What's happened to him?"

"Nothing. He's fine. Perfectly fine. And I really am sorry to bother you like this, but we had a small...problem a few minutes ago."

"A problem?"

"Yes. Mrs. Gates, is Harlan a sleepwalker?"

"Oh, dear, oh, dear. Was he sleepwalking in the hotel?"

"Yes, he was."

"What did she say?" Cade whispered. "Is he?"

Talia nodded a relieved yes. Whatever else Harlan might have been up to tonight, he hadn't climbed over the wall to her balcony for any nefarious purpose.

"Oh, dear," Mrs. Gates said again. "I was afraid of this. He didn't cause any trouble, did he?"

"No, not really. My room is next to his and he...came to my door. But I'm the only one he disturbed. Then I woke the man he's sharing a room with, Cade Hailey."

Cade rolled his eyes and Talia smiled at him. Harlan *had* come to her door. What was there to gain by telling his mother it had been her balcony door? Or that she'd awakened Cade by screaming like a banshee?

"Yes, yes," Mrs. Gates was saying. "Talia and Cade. Harlan talked about both of you while the trial was going on. But you're sure he's all right?"

"He's fine, Mrs. Gates. I just wanted to know if there's anything in particular we should be doing."

"No. Just get him to go back to bed and he'll probably be okay for the rest of the night."

"Well, we've already got him back to bed. But what about after tonight? Is there any way of preventing it from happening again? Any specific thing that triggers the problem?"

"Yes, but there's nothing you can do about it. It's having to sleep in a strange bed. His doctor says it's something to do with anxiety. And being away from home makes him anxious."

"Ah. I see."

"The only other thing we're sure causes it... You don't happen to know if he had anything to drink earlier, do you? Alcohol, I mean?"

"I think he had a beer or two with some of the other jurors."

"Oh, dear, oh, dear. He knows better than to drink. I guess he just wanted to be one of the boys, though. If the others were drinking, I mean."

"Yes, I imagine that was it."

Mrs. Gates sighed loudly. "You know, Harlan's never been in a speck of trouble his entire life. And I'd hate for him to get into any because he's on that jury doing his civic duty."

"I'm sure he'll be fine, Mrs. Gates. And now that we know about his sleepwalking, Cade will be able to keep an eye on him."

"Damn right I'll keep an eye on him," Cade whispered.

"Well, knowing that makes me feel a little better. But I'm sorry he disturbed your sleep, Talia. And tell Cade that, as well, would you?"

"I will. And I'm sorry I disturbed *your* sleep, Mrs. Gates. Good night." Talia hung up and looked at Cade again.

"You don't think she was lying, do you?" he asked. "I mean, if he's not a sleepwalker, the minute you asked about it she'd have realized he'd been up to something."

"No, I don't think she was lying. Most people have no idea what causes sleepwalking, but she did. And she knew the specific things that make Harlan do it."

"Which are?"

"Being away from home, for starters. But tonight was a triple whammy. First he was in the bar drinking, which he's apparently not supposed to do. Then he came back to the room and we upset him with our accusations. Then he had to sleep in a strange bed."

"So the sleepwalking was definitely for real," Cade said. "But we still can't be sure about earlier. About whether he was the guy in the hall."

"No...but his mother said he's never been in a speck of trouble."

"She's his *mother,* Talia."

"True, but we know he can't have any sort of criminal record. If he did he wouldn't have been eligible for jury duty."

When Cade said nothing more Talia simply sat watching him, suddenly struck by the domesticity of the scene. She and Cade sitting together in their bathrobes in the middle of the night. It started her imagining what it would be like to be alone with him in the middle of the night because they'd planned it.

He was rubbing his fingers slowly back and forth on his jaw, clearly lost in thought, and she realized it was the first time she'd seen him needing a shave. It made him look even more masculine. And even more appealing.

She could almost feel that stubble. Feel the rough growth of beard against her fingertips...the granite hardness of his jaw beneath her hand...the warmth of his mouth on hers.

"I wish we knew for sure," he said.

His words jolted her back to reality. "You mean about Harlan? Whether it was him in the hall?"

Cade nodded.

"It seemed perfectly obvious earlier," she said slowly. "But after he denied it so emphatically..."

"He even told me we both owed him an apology—for accusing him."

"Really?"

"Uh-huh. Before he turned in. He said his mother always says people should never go to bed mad."

"That's good advice," Talia murmured, smiling a little. "So did you apologize?"

"Yeah, I did. I figured there was at least a chance we'd been wrong. And if we were he had a right to be mad at us."

When she wearily shook her head, Cade said, "What?"

"Nothing. I mean, nothing new. It's just that we still don't seem to have any answers."

"So you'll just keep being very careful until we do. Everything's going to turn out fine in the end, Talia.

But what about the rest of tonight? My offer to stay right here still goes."

She gazed at him, thinking it had been an extremely tempting offer the first time around. Now it was irresistible. To hell with whatever rumors and innuendoes she might end up facing.

But before she could take him up on it he rose and was saying, "You're right. It's not the greatest idea. So look." He grabbed one of the armchairs. "I'll brace this against the French doors."

He did that, then turned back to her. "The lock's not wonderful, but now nobody can get in without making a helluva racket. The main door's secure, and I'll leave the connecting door unlocked on my side. But I really can't see anything else happening tonight."

"No, I can't imagine anything will." The truth, though, was she could imagine a hundred and one things, each worse than the one before.

When she stood, Cade jammed his hands into the pockets of his robe and took a step backward. "So...I'll see you in the morning."

She nodded, her throat tight. It seemed as if every time they'd been alone together tonight she'd ended up wanting him to kiss her. And she desperately wanted him to now. But he obviously had no intention of doing anything but leaving. He took another step back, and just as he did the truth suddenly hit her—with such blinding clarity she couldn't believe she hadn't seen it long ago.

She'd been misreading his interest in her. Or more accurately, his *lack* of interest. The attraction between them wasn't really *between* them at all. It was completely one-sided. The realization struck like a physical blow, and she simply stared at him, thinking she'd just set a new personal low for not recognizing the obvious.

Over the past six weeks she'd been falling for Cade Hailey. And she'd gone along merrily assuming he was falling for her. But she'd been wrong. Oh, given all the time he'd chosen to spend with her, he had to like her. But liking her as a friend was apparently the extent of it.

"Sleep tight," he said. "And don't forget to lock your side of the door."

She simply nodded again, waiting where she was until he'd gone into his own room. Then she locked up and switched on the television, knowing there was no way in the world she'd be able to sleep tight—or any other way, for that matter.

Turning the volume down to a whisper, she climbed into bed with the remote. The hotel had supplied a television guide, so she checked to see if there were any late-late movies.

When she discovered the only one anywhere near the beginning was *When a Man Loves a Woman,* she pitched the guide across the room and began flipping through the channels, unable to stop wondering what on earth was wrong with her.

The man she'd been busily falling for was only interested in her as a friend. And some man whose identity she didn't know had tried to frighten her to death.

Chapter Eight

As hard as Talia had been trying to concentrate on the deliberations, she realized her eyes had strayed to Cade once more.

Looking away, she wished for the hundredth time that he hadn't plunked himself down next to her in the conference room—just as he'd done every day in the jury box. After she'd tossed and turned all night thinking about him, he was the last person she'd wanted to sit beside this morning.

Of course, she hadn't really been thinking about him *all* night. She'd spent at least half the time conjuring up images of the human monsters that would creep into her room if she dared to fall asleep.

But she shouldn't have been thinking about Cade for even a minute. And she also shouldn't be so upset about misreading his feelings for her. She'd made a mistake. Everybody did that occasionally, and she'd simply mistaken his gestures of friendship for something more.

Or the other possibility, the one that had occurred to her about five in the morning, was that he *had* been falling for her, but had been turned off by the way she'd been acting the last little while. After all, she was usually far better company than she'd been since they'd arrived on the island. Well, to be more specific, since Mrs. Wertman had been shot.

There was nothing like walking in on a murder victim to make your sense of humor desert you and to turn you into miserable company. And that wasn't even taking into account everything that had happened since.

She made another major effort at concentrating and discovered their jury foreman was droning on about something again. The more often he did that the more convinced she grew that they'd made a mistake in selecting him. Although, actually, they *hadn't* selected him. It was more that nobody had objected when he'd volunteered.

"I wouldn't mind doing it," he'd said. "In fact, I'd like to. I spend half my life chairing meetings, so I can keep things on track."

At the time she'd assumed he could. Myron Beyers was in his mid-fifties and the financial vice president of a major corporation. But despite his experience, she'd quickly begun doubting his effectiveness.

Besides talking too much himself, he failed to interrupt when people made blatantly wrong statements about the evidence. She and Cade seemed to have been interrupting far more often than Myron.

She and Cade. Slowly she pushed her hair back from her face, aware that every second thought she had began with *she and Cade.* That had to stop. There *was* no *she and Cade*—never would be. And the sooner she purged her mind of that phrase the better.

When she forced her attention back to the deliberations again, it was Roger Podonyi who was talking. He was holding forth about how Joey Carpaccio hadn't impressed him as the kind of man who'd harm a fly, let alone have someone murder his wife.

"Roger," Cade said at last, "before Joey took the stand his lawyers probably rehearsed him to death. So we really should be concentrating on the evidence, not on our gut feelings about how he came across."

Roger shot Cade a glare he'd undoubtedly perfected with his students. He taught English at a private school, and he obviously wasn't used to being told to shut up—not even as politely as Cade had done it.

"Just take it as a friendly piece of advice, Roger," Myron suggested. "That's the way Cade meant it."

"Advice is worth what you pay for it," Roger muttered. "And there's a lot to be said for gut feelings."

Talia agreed with that, although Roger wouldn't be happy if he knew what her gut feelings were about him. Forty or so, tall and fit, Roger seemed easygoing enough most of the time. But she sensed an underlying violence, much like what she saw in some of the abusive husbands she dealt with. She was sure he had a mean streak tucked away beneath the surface.

At the very least, he clearly felt Joey's wife had deserved what she'd gotten, which made him one of the defense team's jury-selection triumphs.

When Myron checked his watch, then began summing up what they'd covered in the morning's session, Talia glanced slowly along the length of the table, letting her gaze linger on each of the other jurors in turn.

She still hadn't figured out which one of the others had voted guilty yesterday, although a few of them had made it apparent that they were on the not-guilty side of the fence.

"Well," Myron said as her gaze reached him once more, "it's about time to break for lunch. So let's meet back here at one-thirty."

"I'll say it's about time," Cade whispered to her. "I'm starving."

She didn't have to look at him to know he was expecting to eat with her. They always ate together. But now that she knew how she'd misinterpreted his attentions, she didn't feel exactly comfortable with him.

What they needed was a buffer, so she caught Harlan's eye and asked if he'd like to join them. They were on good terms again—reasonably good terms at least—because the first thing she'd done at breakfast was apologize for accusing him last night.

Good terms or not, though, he wasn't interested in lunch.

"I really have to go up to the room and phone my mom," he said. "I should've called her first thing this morning, because Cade said she was awfully worried when you talked to her last night."

Talia nodded, suddenly feeling guilty about not phoning her own parents this morning. From the start they'd been concerned about her being on the Carpaccio jury. And by now, with Mrs. Wertman's murder undoubtedly the top news story in Charleston, they'd be nervous wrecks. Deciding she'd better call them right after lunch, she turned her attention back to Harlan.

"And aside from phoning Mom," he was saying, "I didn't get much time on my computer yesterday. So I thought I'd just grab a bag of chips from the guest shop and cruise the information highway for an hour. But maybe we'll do lunch tomorrow? If we're still here?"

"Sure. Sounds good."

Harlan pushed his thick glasses up his nose and gave her a chipmunk grin. Then he hurried off to do his phoning and cruising.

"Looks like it's just you and me," Cade said.

She nodded, but with any luck some of the other jurors would have a couple of empty chairs at their table.

CADE HEADED SILENTLY for the dining room with Talia, barely able to resist the urge to reach for her hand.

Last night he'd wanted her so badly he'd used up every last bit of his self-control. So now he was running on empty, and he had to talk to her about *them* as soon as possible.

Hell, he'd practically cheered when Harlan opted for spending the lunch break on the information highway, because it meant they could talk right now, which was perfect.

Unlike last night, he was sure she'd be thinking straight. And he…well, he was *reasonably* sure he was thinking straight.

Oh, his brain was still warning him about not making the same mistake twice, but he'd decided his brain was just being overly cautious. There *were* similarities between Talia and his ex-wife, but only a few. And a pretty superficial few at that.

So what was the point in even trying to pretend he wasn't crazy about Talia? He just couldn't see one any longer. But he could sure see a point in letting her know how he felt. When he'd held her last night, when she'd snuggled close to him, all soft and warm… He didn't stop his thoughts from drifting along that track, and by the time they reached the dining room he was practically walking on air.

"It looks as if the sheriff's people have completely cleared out," Talia said while they waited for the maître d' to appear.

The sheriff's people were the last thing on Cade's mind, but he looked around and saw that she was right. He'd noticed a few of them at breakfast, but there was no sign of them now.

Absently he wondered if they'd gotten anywhere close to catching the murderer. Then he spotted the maître d' heading toward them and turned his thoughts to how he should begin his conversation with Talia.

"A table for two?" the maître d' asked.

"Well, actually—" Talia began.

"That'd be fine," Cade said.

When they started across the room, he felt as if a weight had just been lifted off his shoulders. In a few more minutes he'd have his cards laid out on that little table for two.

Then the familiar voice of Bud the baby-sitter called, "Talia? Cade? Come join us."

The maître d' stopped and glanced questioningly back at them. Cade looked in the direction Bud's voice had come from. The court officer was smiling expectantly at them from a table for four. Only Bud's and the chair opposite his were occupied.

"That's fine," Talia said before he had a chance to open his mouth.

Then she and the maître d' changed course, and all he could do was follow along. As they neared the table the fellow sitting with Bud rose politely. He appeared to be in his mid-thirties and was unquestionably one of the resort guests. Tall and blond, he was dressed casually but expensively. The practiced smile he flashed their way was clearly designed to make people like him.

While the maître d' deposited menus at the two vacant places, Bud got to his feet, as well, even though he didn't normally display grade-A manners. "Talia, Cade," he said, "I'd like you to meet Gerald Asimov."

"Gerr," the guy said, extending his hand to each of them in turn. "My friends call me Gerr."

"Asimov?" Talia said. "Do people always ask if you're related to Isaac Asimov?"

Gerr gave a self-deprecating shrug. "Yes they always ask, and I really wish I was. Maybe it would make my books sell better."

"Oh, you're a writer, as well?" she asked.

Her fascinated expression made Cade decide he wasn't any too crazy about Gerr.

"Well, actually I'm a lawyer." Gerr pulled Talia's chair out for her. "But I write, too."

"Really. You can't have much spare time then."

Gerr shook his head. "I practice criminal law in New York City. So I spend most of my days in courtrooms and most of my nights writing."

"And it's fiction you write?" Talia asked.

"Uh-huh. Legal thrillers. But I'd really rather not listen to myself talk, so I'm glad you could join us.

"Both of you," he added, smiling at Cade. "Bud was just saying he hoped the two of you would be coming in here with the others."

"Oh?" Cade casually opened his menu.

"Gerr asked the Judge to introduce him to me this morning," Bud explained, "because he wanted to talk to some of the jurors. But he didn't think he should just approach anyone directly. And I said I thought you two would be good people to start with."

Gerr nodded. "You see, the book I'm working on right now has a murder trial in it. But I'm trying a different twist, and I'm having a rough go of it. That's why I'm here. I finally decided I had to get away from everything and take time to find the right perspective. So yesterday morning I grabbed my laptop, checked out of my office and flew down to Charleston."

For a guy who'd rather not listen to himself talk, Cade thought blackly, old Gerr wasn't exactly Silent Sam.

"He packed up and flew down here just like that," Bud was saying.

Gerr laughed. "It wasn't quite 'just like that,' Bud. I had to do some major rescheduling before I could get away. And find a place to stay.

"I was actually booked into the Planter's Inn," he continued, naming one of the most expensive hotels in Charleston, "but the fellow I was sitting next to on the flight told me about Bride's Bay."

"The Planter's a nice place, too," Bud offered.

"Yeah, so I heard. But this sounded like just what I wanted. So I called right then and there from the plane, and as luck would have it they had a vacancy. All I had to do was find a boat at the harbor to bring me over."

"Then the next thing he knew," Bud said, "he was in the middle of something he'll be able to use in a book."

"Could be," Gerr agreed. "I'd only been here a couple of hours when that woman was murdered. And was I glad I'd switched hotels then. I mean who could ask for anything better?"

"Than a murder?" Cade said dryly.

"Oh, I don't mean I was glad the poor woman got killed. It's just that writers have a different outlook on experiences like that than most people. So I found it . . . interesting. Then somebody told me there was a murder-trial jury sequestered here, and I just couldn't believe my good luck. You see, what's been giving me so much trouble with my book is that I'm slanting it from the point of view of a juror, and—"

"And he's never been a juror," Bud interrupted. "Because lawyers aren't eligible to serve on juries."

"Right. I've always been on the courtroom floor during trials. I mean, I've certainly coached witnesses on how jurors will perceive them, but I need to get a handle on the psychological nuances of being on the other side of the jury box. So I thought if I could just talk to some of you people one-on-one..."

Gerald-call-me-Gerr paused to flash Talia a smile that made Cade nauseous.

"And," he went on, "when Bud told me you're a psychologist, Talia, I figured you'd be ideal—very perceptive about the sort of thing I'm after."

"We're not allowed to discuss the trial," Cade pointed out. "As a lawyer, you must know that."

Gerr glanced at him. "Oh, of course. I don't intend to talk specifically about the Carpaccio trial. That's not what I'm interested in. It's the psychological experience of knowing you'll be deciding a man's fate. Especially in a state that has the death penalty. I'd like to hear your feelings on the matter, as well, Cade. It's just that when Bud told me Talia was a psychologist..."

His gaze returned to her. "As I said, I assume your insights would be particularly helpful."

"Am I allowed to discuss that sort of thing?" Talia asked Bud.

"Like I told you earlier," Gerr said, turning to Bud, "I don't want to get you into any trouble over this."

Bud laughed. "And like I told you, I'm due to retire next year. The worse trouble I could get is an early pension, and I sure wouldn't complain about that." He glanced at Talia. "But I don't see any problem," he said. "Not as long as you talk in generalities. Just steer clear of anything specifically related to the Carpaccio evidence."

She nodded, then looked at Gerr again. "Well, I don't know how much help I'll be, but I can certainly give it a try."

Gerr positively beamed at her. "Shall we say over dinner tonight?"

Cade stared pointedly at his menu. During the long silence that ensued he could feel Talia's eyes on him. He didn't glance up, though. If she wanted to have dinner with this guy, instead of with him, it was entirely up to her.

"Yes," she finally murmured. "Dinner tonight would be fine."

WHEN TALIA'S GAZE wandered to the door connecting her room and Cade's, she forced it away and told herself to concentrate on getting ready for dinner. Whatever Mr. Hailey's problem was, it was of no real interest to her.

She'd had a lot of time now to get her head organized—more than enough to realize that thinking she'd been falling in love with him had been plain crazy. Which meant his only liking her as a friend was no problem at all. In fact, it was just as well. Because that was exactly how she felt about him.

Zipping up her dress, she tried to force the word *denial* from her mind. She was *not* in denial. Nor was she rationalizing. She'd simply put things into their proper perspective and was seeing them more realistically than she had before. And since she wasn't interested in Cade, the reason for his sulking didn't matter to her.

She glanced at the connecting door again, thinking she merely found it curious that he'd been acting so strangely all afternoon. Why, he'd barely said a word to her since she'd agreed to have dinner with Gerald Asimov. It was almost as if there was a little jealousy at work, but that couldn't be his problem.

Whatever was going on, though, she had no intention of giving Cade Hailey another thought. As of this very instant he was a closed subject. She'd simply go downstairs and enjoy dinner. And enjoy talking with someone other than Cade for a change.

"Dammit," she muttered. So much for not giving him another thought. The way he kept popping into her mind every two seconds was getting darned annoying.

She glanced at the bedside clock and saw there was a good half hour before she was supposed to meet Gerr. But before she could think about how to fill the time, someone knocked on her door. Her sixth sense told her it was Cade, and her pulse gave a funny little skip.

She resisted muttering a second "dammit," but either her brain had forgotten to tell her pulse that she wasn't interested in him, or her pulse was on the fritz.

Her sixth sense, she discovered by checking the peephole, was on the fritz, as well. It wasn't Cade standing in the hall. It was Detective Frank Boscoe.

When she opened the door he gave her his cool version of a warm smile, then asked if he could come in. "I have something important to talk to you about," he said.

"Of course." She stepped back to let him pass, then closed the door again and eyed him expectantly.

"I've come to tell you," he said, "where things stand with Mrs. Wertman's murder."

Chapter Nine

The mention of Mrs. Wertman's murder sent a chill down Talia's spine. After spending the entire day in that conference room, concentrating on the details surrounding Maria Carpaccio's death, she'd been doing her best to block thoughts of both murders from her mind.

"It's rather unorthodox," Frank Boscoe said, "to give you information about a case in progress. But I came back over here to fill the Judge in personally—as a professional courtesy. And he asked me to extend the courtesy to you, To relieve your mind."

She nodded, glad the Judge had been thinking of her, because she had a feeling Boscoe would have rather just left her in the dark.

"Now, this is still confidential. We haven't issued a statement to the media yet, so I need your assurance you won't repeat anything."

"All right. You've got my word."

"Good. Then you'll be glad to hear we have the killers in custody. And that the murder had absolutely nothing to do with you."

Even though he sounded certain, she was almost afraid to believe he was right. "Killers," she finally said. "Plural?"

"Uh-huh. Two of them. The shooter and the person who hired him. The boys on the mainland wrapped things up a few hours ago, and it turned out we were just spinning our wheels over here. The shooter was in a powerboat heading back to Charleston ten minutes after the murder."

"It was a planned hit then," she said, slipping into the jargon that had become far too familiar lately.

Boscoe nodded. "The shooter's a pro. We only got him because the other perp broke down and confessed."

"And . . . you're positive you've got the right people?"

"Absolutely. It was Mrs. Wertman's daughter who planned things."

Talia felt as if someone had struck her. "Her daughter?" she whispered.

"Uh-huh. Ruth Wertman was a wealthy divorcée. And her twenty-two-year-old daughter was named as her sole heir."

"My Lord," Talia murmured, "it sounds like a replay of the Menendez brothers."

"Same idea."

Talia shook her head. Even with her overactive imagination, she could no more imagine hiring someone to kill her own mother than she could imagine being an aardvark.

"It really stinks, doesn't it?" Boscoe muttered. "But at least you can be sure you're safe."

"Yes . . . yes, thank you for letting me know," she said slowly, trying to think if there were any loose ends she should ask about while she had the chance.

"But the room," she finally said. "Why was the killer waiting in the room *I'd* been assigned?"

"He wasn't. Not originally. He started off here—in the room they'd intended for Mrs. Wertman."

Talia swallowed uneasily, imagining him here, touching things she'd touched. Quickly she forced her attention back to Boscoe.

"But when she got up here," he was saying, "and decided she had to have a different room, our friend followed her back down to the lobby. Then he hung around within earshot of the desk."

"He followed her down to the lobby just like that? Without either her or Shad Teach noticing?"

Boscoe shrugged. "Like I said, the guy's a pro, so I guess he just faded right into the woodwork. Then as soon as he heard they were switching her to 203, he came back upstairs and slipped its lock."

"I just can't believe it," Talia whispered.

"Well, that's what happened. He came here to do a job, did it and cleared out. Which means that your guy in the hall last night was exactly what Rebuzo and I figured—just some weirdo."

For a second, knowing that for sure made her feel a little better. But only for a second. Because whoever the weirdo was, he was likely still around.

When she raised the likelihood of that, Boscoe nodded. "I'm afraid he probably is. And I'm also afraid we don't have the manpower to do anything about him. We just can't justify leaving any of our people on the island."

"Then I'm on my own?"

"Not entirely. The Judge said they'll have security keeping a close watch out for anything suspicious. Just in case."

"Yes . . . well, I guess that's better than nothing."

"I'm sorry we can't do more for you," Boscoe said, opening the door to leave. "But as long as you're careful, everything should be okay."

"Yes. Of course." She stood watching until he reached the end of the hall, then glanced at Cade's door, wishing she could tell him what she'd just learned. But she'd promised she wouldn't say a word. And the way he'd been acting, he probably wouldn't care, anyway.

Closing the door, she wandered across the room and stood gazing out over the ocean—glad the sheriff's department had solved the case and had its murderers locked up, but hardly thrilled that her own personal weirdo was still on the loose.

"THIS WAS A REAL GOOD idea," Harlan said, polishing off the final chunk of his steak.

"Yeah," Cade muttered.

He sat staring morosely at the flickering candle on the room-service table. This was a really good idea all right. Practically his dream come true. Eating dinner in the room with Harlan, while Talia was downstairs enjoying herself with Gerald-call-me-Gerr.

But at least this way he didn't have to watch them. He shoved his plate to one side and reached for the carafe of coffee.

"So, how come you're not eating with Talia tonight?" Harlan asked.

Cade shrugged.

"You have a fight with her?"

"No, nothing like that."

Harlan glanced over at the screen saver floating on his laptop, then focused on Cade again, an inquisitive expression on his pale face. Cade swore to himself. The room was equipped with a dedicated line for computer and fax equipment, and Harlan had been talking—or was it typing?—to someone in California before dinner.

He'd said he was going to connect with another of his computer buddies right after they'd eaten, so if he was more interested in what had happened with Talia than in logging back onto the Internet, he probably wouldn't just let the subject drop.

"There's some lawyer-cum-writer staying at the hotel who wanted to talk to her," Cade said, trying to fill Harlan in as concisely as possible. "So they're having dinner together."

"Yeah? What did he want to talk to her about?"

Briefly Cade explained.

"So is this guy a famous writer or what?"

"No idea. I've never heard of him, but that doesn't count for much."

"Want me to find out? If he's well-known, I mean?"

"Can you do that?"

"Sure. I can plug into the catalogs of a zillion different libraries. Want me to give it a shot?"

Cade shrugged. He didn't particularly want to learn old Gerr had written a dozen books that were in every public library in North America. But surely, if the guy was a best-selling author, Cade had read enough crime fiction that he'd have recognized the name. And he wouldn't mind hearing Gerr was a complete unknown.

"What the hell," he finally said, "let's go for it. His name's Gerald Asimov."

Harlan headed over to his bed and settled in with his laptop once more. Cade sat half-watching his roommate, half-wondering if Gerr had anything more than talking to Talia on his mind. He didn't like the thought of that. Didn't like it at all.

But there wasn't a thing he could do about it—except kick himself for spending six entire weeks being a damn fool, playing his dumb look-but-don't-touch game.

"Nothing," Harlan said after a couple of minutes.

"What?"

"Nothing. I've checked four different libraries, and none of them have a listing for an author named Gerald Asimov."

Cade couldn't help smiling a little. He liked Harlan's news flash. "So he's not exactly Elmore Leonard."

"Who?"

"A really well-known crime writer."

"Oh. No, I guess not. Not unless he uses a pseudonym."

Cade's grin faded. "Can you find out?"

"Yeah, I think so." Harlan went back to his keyboarding for another minute or two, then said, "We're going to have to wait."

Cade shot him a curious glance.

"I think," Harlan explained, "the Library of Congress cross-references pseudonyms. But the data base is down. They're probably updating it or something. So, you want me to check any more catalogs?"

"No, don't bother. But look, I'm feeling kind of restless, so I think I'll head down to the bar for a while. You want to come?"

Harlan had taken a shower after the day's deliberations and was wearing only his kung fu pajamas. He wasn't likely to want to go anywhere, but it seemed only polite to ask.

He shook his head. "After last night there's no way I'd go to the bar. In fact, I'm not leaving this room again till morning. I just want to talk to my buddy in Arizona."

Cade nodded and blew out the candle. He'd been wanting to do that from the moment the waiter lit it. There was something about it that really annoyed him. Probably, he silently admitted, it was because he equated candlelight dinners with romantic evenings. And if anyone was having a romantic evening, it sure wasn't him.

He glanced at the door that led to Talia's room, hoping it wasn't her and old Gerr, either.

That thought preying on his mind, he headed downstairs to the bar. When he walked in, four of the other jurors were sitting around one of the larger coffee tables.

He pulled up a chair to join them and got three friendly greetings. What he got from Roger Podonyi, though, was a surly grunt. Since their resident English teacher was normally talkative, he figured Roger was still steamed about being told to concentrate on the evidence, not his gut feelings.

A few minutes later, when another of the other jurors wandered in and headed in their direction, Roger announced he was going for a walk.

"I'm going to pack it in, too," Myron Beyers, their jury foreman, said. He lingered after he stood up, though, until Roger was gone. Then he looked over at Cade.

"Hey," he said quietly. "I'm rooming with Roger, you know."

Cade grinned. "Lucky you." That almost ranked with having Harlan for a roommate.

"Yeah, one day, and I've heard his entire life story. But take a friendly piece of advice, Cade. Maybe you shouldn't get him any angrier at you."

"No?"

"No, it could be dangerous. He doesn't just teach English at that ritzy private school. He's a crack shot, and he coaches students on the shooting range."

Cade waited for some sign that Myron was joking. When it didn't come he said, "I'm probably safe enough. I doubt he brought his gun along...did he?"

Myron shrugged. "I haven't seen one, but maybe he did. He mentioned the resort has a shooting range. And that he's planning on hitting it when he gets a chance."

"Great," Cade muttered. "If I turn up dead make sure you mention all that to the cops, will you?"

TALIA LEANED BACK, sipping her final few drops of wine while Gerald switched off his tiny tape recorder and stuck it into his suit pocket.

All the jurors who'd been in the dining room had been wearing casual clothes, but the majority of the resort guests had dressed for dinner—and dressed extremely well. Gerr's suit was obviously not off the rack.

"Was I any help?" she asked when he met her gaze again.

"You were great. I'm already feeling a lot better about the book." He gave her a smile she found a touch unsettling.

He seemed like a nice enough guy, but he was a little too smooth and polished for her liking. And even though he hadn't said a word to suggest he had any interest in her—other than as an interviewee—she had a feeling he wasn't a man who enjoyed finding himself alone in bed at the end of an evening.

"It's an hypnotic sound, isn't it?" he said.

For a minute she wasn't sure what he meant. Then she realized that since they'd stopped talking the faint crashing of waves was audible.

"Very peaceful," she murmured, glancing out into the night. The candle on their table was casting a glow on the dark glass, and their images were framed in the window.

Beyond that, she could see across the groomed hotel grounds to the road. On the far side, the beach stretched silver in the moonlight, and moonbeams danced on the white froth of the Atlantic surf.

"I love being near the water," Gerr told her. "I've got a summer place in Cape Cod, and I head up there every time I can escape."

She merely nodded. Remarks like that always made her feel sorry for people who lived in the Big Apple. It seemed that every New Yorker she'd ever met talked in terms of escaping from the city.

"How about a walk on the beach?" Gerr suggested. "I was out just before dinner and it wasn't too chilly."

"Oh...no, I'm wearing this dress...and heels, so—"

"You could change. After being locked up in that conference room all day, some fresh air would do you good."

"Well..." She glanced outside again. He was right. A little fresh air *would* do her good. And if it was Cade suggesting they go for a walk, she knew she'd jump at the idea. But why on earth was she thinking about Cade again?

"Hey," Gerr teased, "I'm a lawyer and writer, not a rapist and murderer. But I guess until the police get that killer you're going to be pretty nervous."

"Yes, I guess that's it."

They already had the killer, though. Thanks to Frank Boscoe, she knew that. And there wasn't any real reason to be leery of Gerald Asimov. He was far too cool to try anything she couldn't handle.

"But being nervous is silly, isn't it?" she said, deciding. "So, why don't I just run upstairs and change. It'll only take me two minutes to put on jeans and sneakers."

Gerr smiled. "Good. I think I'll get into something more comfortable, too. Gucci didn't design his shoes for walking on the beach."

Once he'd signed the bill they headed for the second floor. When they reached the top of the stairs, Gerr started to turn left, then hesitated, seeing that she was turning right. "I'll walk you to your room."

"Oh, no, I'm fine. Really. I'll meet you in the lobby in a few minutes."

"Uh-uh. Bud mentioned you're probably worried about more than that woman's murder. He told me what happened last night—about the guy with the gun. So let's not give him a chance at a repeat performance."

She nodded, telling herself there was a fine line between being brave and being foolish. And insisting on walking to her room alone when she'd be scared spitless doing it was decidedly foolish. Despite her anxiety, though, their trip down the hall was uneventful.

"You're okay going in by yourself?" Gerr asked as she unlocked her door.

"Uh-huh. I'll see you downstairs in five minutes." She flicked on her light, then glanced back and smiled. "See? No murderers."

When he laughed, she forced another smile. Then she closed the door and glanced toward the balcony.

The maid had cleaned earlier, putting everything where it belonged—including the chair Cade had braced against the balcony doors last night. No doubt the woman had strict instructions about how she was to leave the room.

But the bed was already turned down, with two chocolate truffles perched enticingly on the pillow, so the maid wouldn't be in again until tomorrow. And that meant there was no reason not to put the chair back where it would make things safer.

After moving it Talia started for the bathroom, unzipping her dress as she walked. With each step, her heart beat faster.

She firmly told herself that was ridiculous. There was no killer waiting in her bathroom. The sheriff's people had him securely locked away.

Stopping at the door, she gingerly pushed it open and reached inside for the light—not quite able to erase her mental image of Mrs. Wertman lying in a spreading pool of blood. Then she flicked the switch and the light flashed on, revealing nothing but the shiny white bathroom.

Her heartbeat began to slow. Ridiculous or not, seeing the room was empty was a relief. Muttering that she was becoming downright paranoid, she changed and hurried back downstairs. When she got to the lobby Gerr was already there, chatting with Judge Bradshaw.

As she reached them, the Judge finished whatever he was saying to Gerr and turned to her. "Frank Boscoe spoke to you, I trust?"

"Yes. Thank you for asking him to."

He nodded. "Well, Gerr said you were off for a walk, and I don't want to hold you up. I've got to find Liz, anyway, so I'd best get back to looking for her."

Talia smiled a goodbye, then headed outside with Gerr. The night was just cool enough to be refreshing, and the moment she smelled the sea breeze she was glad she'd decided to come. Gerr had been right. After being cooped up all day, this was exactly what she needed.

They walked until they reached the road that paralleled the shore, then turned left—toward the north end of the island where the private estates and village were. After following the road for a few hundred yards, they cut down onto the beach and began walking not far from the water's edge.

"This reminds me of the Cape," Gerr said, breaking the silence. "Of course, it's cooler up there in April, but most of the bite's gone from the wind, so you know summer's on the way."

Talia nodded, taking another deep breath of the fresh sea air and wondering why she'd been so nervous about the idea of coming out. She really must be at risk of becoming paranoid.

Gerald Asimov had wanted to go for a walk, period. Any man with an ulterior motive would have at least tried to take her hand by this point.

"Which of the other jurors do you think I should talk to?" he asked. "Which of them are most perceptive?"

"Cade Hailey," she said automatically.

"Yeah? Bud mentioned he'd probably be helpful, but he didn't seem too friendly at lunch."

"I think he just had something on his mind."

"Okay, then I'll try to set something up with him and—"

Suddenly there was a series of sharp spitting sounds in the sand near their feet and a sound like a car backfiring again and again.

Confused, Talia looked toward the empty road, trying to see where the car was.

Before she could spot it, Gerr grabbed her arm and roughly dragged her down behind a huge driftwood log.

Terrified, she tried to struggle up.

He shoved her back down, hissing, "Don't move! Somebody's shooting at us!"

Chapter Ten

Crouching behind the hulking chunk of driftwood with Gerald Asimov, Talia desperately wished she could crawl into the sand and disappear. The best she could do, though, was try not to move a muscle.

They hadn't heard a sound from their shooter in several endless seconds. But given the crashing of the waves and the pounding of her heart that didn't mean a thing. He could be closing in for the kill right this instant, and they'd never hear him.

But who was he? Her weirdo? Or had Ruth Wertman's murderer returned? Or maybe he'd never left. Maybe the cops had arrested the wrong people.

"There he goes now," Gerr whispered.

"Wait!" she cried as he scrambled to his feet and started sprinting across the beach. Her plea was lost in the roar of the ocean.

Frozen by fear and indecision, she followed Gerr with her eyes. Then she looked past him, spotted the man he'd seen and felt a faint sense of relief.

He hadn't been closing in for the kill at all. He was running away—simply a dark figure running along the road. But Gerr was angling across the beach after him, which was crazy. He was liable to get himself shot.

As she watched, someone else appeared in the distance, coming rapidly from the direction of the hotel. Even with only the moonlight to see by, she recognized his stride. It was Cade. And the shooter was running toward him. When they rounded the bend in the road they'd come face-to-face.

For a moment her heart stopped. Then she pushed herself up from the cold sand and started racing across it. If that guy started shooting again Cade could end up dead.

Her throat tight, she tried to run faster, cursing the sand for slowing her down. Ahead she saw the shooter and Cade nearing each other, and her heart almost stopped again. But there was no more shooting. Once the two men reached each other, they stopped and began to talk. Then Gerr reached them and gestured in her direction.

Cade started charging across the sand toward her. When he wordlessly folded her into his arms she clung to him, her knees suddenly so weak she didn't know how she'd managed to stand, let alone run.

"You okay?" he murmured.

She nodded against his chest, fighting off threatening tears. How could she have even tried to convince herself she didn't feel anything special for him? The man who'd been shooting at her was standing right up there on the road, yet she felt absurdly safe in Cade's arms.

"What are you doing here?" she asked at last.

"Making sure you're okay. That's what friends are for." He gently smoothed her windblown hair with his fingers. The gesture was so tender she almost lost the battle and gave in to her tears.

"I was in the bar," he said, "and the Judge came in looking for Liz. He mentioned you'd gone out for a walk with old Gerr and I just... Oh, hell, Talia, I just wanted to make sure you were all right. I mean you don't really know anything about the guy, so..."

"Thank you," she whispered.

"You're welcome," he whispered back. Then he simply held her close while his heartbeat began to slow a little.

He'd never been more terrified than when he'd heard that gunfire up ahead. He'd known she was out here someplace, and all he'd been able to think was that he could lose her. Lose her before she was even his to lose.

"There was really no reason to worry about Gerr," she murmured at last, then pointed toward the road. "But, oh, Cade, that man there was shooting at us."

"No, it wasn't him. That's Roger Podonyi." Reluctantly he released his hold and glanced across the sand to where Roger and Gerr were waiting.

"Roger? I...I didn't recognize him. But if it wasn't him...Cade, *somebody* was shooting at us. And a minute later Roger was running away."

"I know. But he said he didn't know what the hell was going on. If the guy who killed Mrs. Wertman is still around, though, maybe—"

"No. No, it wasn't him, either. For a minute I was thinking that, too, but it couldn't've been him. I talked to Frank Boscoe before dinner, and they've got Ruth Wertman's murderer locked up."

Cade listened while she briefly filled in the details. "Then it obviously wasn't him," he said when she finished.

"And you're sure about Roger?"

"Hell, Talia, there's damn little I'm sure about at the moment. But he said he was only running because he figured this wasn't exactly a safe place to be. He didn't even realize you and Gerr were on the beach."

"But how could he not have seen us? We were walking right out in the open."

"I don't know. I only spoke to him for a second. But let's not worry about that right now. Let's just get the hell out of here. We're like sitting ducks in the moonlight."

They started across the sand, Cade's mind racing. From the moment he'd heard those shots, his only thought had been for Talia's safety. But now that he knew she was all right, he'd begun thinking about what Myron Beyers had told him—that Roger didn't just teach English, that he was a crack shot who taught some of his students to shoot.

So maybe Roger *did* know what had been going on. After all, as Talia had just said, how could he not have seen them when they were right out in the open? By the time they made it to the road, he was almost convinced it *was* Roger who'd been doing the shooting— and almost ready to kill him with his bare hands.

"You're sure you didn't see the guy with the gun, Roger?" he demanded as they reached him and Gerr.

"What kind of question is that? If I had I'd have told you."

Cade shrugged, trying not to lose his cool entirely. "It just seems kind of hard to believe. I mean, you must have known roughly where the shots were coming from. And if there was someone standing there, I don't understand how you didn't—"

"*If* there was someone standing there?" Roger snapped. "What's that supposed to mean? That you think there might not have been? That you think it was me? Dammit, Hailey, you can be a real pain. Do I smell like I've fired a gun recently?" he asked, shoving his palms practically against Cade's nose. "If I had, there'd be gunpowder residue on my hands. You'd be able to smell the cordite."

"He's right, Cade," Gerr said quietly.

Cade nodded, telling himself to take it easy. Roger *was* right, which meant he couldn't be their shooter. "Sorry, Roger," he muttered. "I wasn't thinking straight. Of course it wasn't you."

"But who was it?" Talia murmured.

Cade turned to her. Her eyes were luminous, and she looked so frightened that he desperately wished he could come up with an answer to her question. Before it was too late.

JUST AS THE FOUR OF THEM started the trek back to the resort, the beam of headlights appeared on the road behind them. Seconds later, one of the hotel minivans caught up with them.

When the driver pulled alongside and leaned across to the open passenger window, it took Talia a second to realize the person at the wheel was Liz Jermain.

Normally the hotel manager was the picture of composure. Even when she'd been confronted with a dead body Liz hadn't entirely lost her equanimity. But at the moment her hair was mussed, her face flushed, and she looked decidedly flustered.

"Are any of you tired of walking?" she asked. "I can give you a lift the rest of the way back if you'd like."

"That's probably a good idea," Cade said. He slid the back door open and gestured Talia inside. "There's been some trouble," he added, climbing in after her.

"Oh, no," Liz said, smoothing her hair. "Please tell me it was nothing as serious as Mrs. Wertman's murder."

"It could have been," Gerr muttered, climbing into the front with her. "Talia and I were walking along the beach and somebody opened fire on us."

"Oh, my God. You're sure it was you that—"

"Positive. If his aim had been any better we'd be dead meat."

"Oh, my God," she said again. "And nobody from security's shown up?"

"With the direction of the wind," Roger said, "nobody at the hotel would've heard the shots."

"No," Liz said. "No, I guess you're right. But, Lord, I thought we had that problem sorted out for good."

"What problem?" Cade asked.

Liz shifted into drive and started off before she answered. "This has happened a couple of times before," she finally told them. "I don't mean he's ever actually shot at *people* before—just coons—but if he thought you were out there looking for eggs . . ."

"Looking for what?" Roger said.

"I think," Liz said, "I'd better back up and explain from the beginning."

Cade reached for Talia's hand in the darkness and gave it a reassuring squeeze. "At least there *is* an explanation," he whispered, his lips so close to her ear that the warmth of his breath ignited a tiny flame deep within her.

"It's one of the estate owners," Liz said as Talia tried to ignore the way that flame began to lick at her belly.

"All of them are wealthy," Liz continued, "and they've gone through life doing pretty well whatever they pleased. I guess that's one of the things they like about the island. There's an attitude of 'live and let live' here, so nobody bothers them about their eccentricities. But...well, one fellow we call the Colonel has developed Alzheimer's. And he's always had a thing about the island's raccoons because—"

"Liz," Talia interrupted quietly, "whoever was shooting wasn't aiming at any raccoon. Gerr wasn't exaggerating about how close the shots came. I could see them hitting the sand by our feet.''

Liz shook her head. ''I don't know what to say. The Judge will have to talk to the Colonel's wife again. She's already hired a live-in nurse, but I guess even the two of them can't watch him twenty-four hours a day.''

''So he sometimes just wanders around the island with a gun?'' Cade said.

''No...no, it hasn't happened in ages. But you see, like a lot of the Sea Islands, Jermain Island is a nesting place for loggerhead turtles. And for as long as I can remember...'' Liz paused to negotiate the turn off the main road.

''For as long as I can remember,'' she began again, ''the Colonel's been concerned about their preservation. Every year, he'd organize patrols on the beach when the eggs were hatching to keep the birds from getting the hatchlings before they could make it into the water.''

She pulled the minivan to a stop in front of the hotel, then turned to finish her story. ''But about ten years ago the island's raccoon population had gotten so large they were eating most of the eggs. That made the Colonel declare his own personal war on them. And now that he's so confused . . .''

''You're trying to tell us,'' Gerr said, ''he's so senile that he mistook Talia and me for giant raccoons out after turtle eggs?''

Liz gave an unhappy shrug. ''The turtles don't even lay their eggs until summer. And I'm sure he knew you werc people. But he must have assumed you were after eggs and…well, as I said, the Judge will talk to the man's wife again. She's going to have to hire a second nurse or something, because he's obviously gotten downright dangerous. There's no other explanation for what happened.''

Talia glanced at Cade, wondering if he could think of any other explanation. *She* certainly could. And it had nothing to do with a senile Colonel and raccoons and turtle eggs. It had to do with her own personal, and still unidentified, weirdo.

''I'll speak to the Judge about this immediately,'' Liz said as her passengers started to pile out. ''I'm just going to put the van away, then I'll go and talk to him. I'm sure he'll call the Colonel's wife tonight.''

''Yes…well,'' Talia murmured, stepping down to the driveway, ''I'd like to know what she has to say.''

''I'll make sure you do,'' Liz promised.

''Talia?'' Gerr said when she turned from the van. ''Roger and I are just going to talk about something for a couple of minutes. Do you want to wait for me in the lobby?''

''No, that's all right. Cade's room is right next to mine, so I'll get home safely.''

Cade draped his arm over her shoulders, wordlessly assuring her she would, then quietly said, ''Do you think it could be the senile Colonel?''

''Well, I did wonder if Liz was jumping to conclusions.''

"Yeah? Well, I wondered if she was doing a lot more than that. What do you figure she was up to, out there on the road at this time of night?"

Talia drew a complete blank. "I don't know. It's too late for her to have been in the village. Nothing would be open. But maybe she was visiting someone in the estates. She's probably friends with some of the people who live there."

"Yeah, I guess that could be it. But whatever she was doing, the Judge didn't know about it. From what he said when he was looking for her, he assumed she was somewhere in the hotel. And did you notice how she looked when she stopped to pick us up?"

Talia nodded, a little wave of anxiety washing over her. "She was awfully flushed and windblown, wasn't she."

"I'll say. As if she might have been running... or maybe shooting."

TALIA MADE A QUICK TRIP into the washroom off the lobby, and when she came back out Cade was talking to Joanie, the concierge.

Rather than interrupt, she stood waiting for him to finish—and thinking about him. Thinking about the way he'd raced across the beach and taken her in his arms. Thinking how cherished that had made her feel.

She was trying with all her might *not* to think about it, though, because the feeling of being cherished was gone now, replaced by a sense of total devastation. After she'd worked so hard to convince herself she didn't care about him, his embrace had forced her to face reality. And this particular reality was awfully tough to face.

She'd fallen in love with Cade. More deeply and completely in love than she'd ever thought possible. But he hadn't fallen in love with her.

She glanced longingly at the staircase, thinking how much she'd like to go up to her room and have a good therapeutic cry. But under the circumstances, she couldn't even allow herself the luxury of wallowing in self-pity. Not for the moment at least. What she had to do right now—unless she wanted to end up dead, instead of merely a victim of unrequited love—was figure out who'd been shooting at her.

Of course it was always possible Gerald Asimov had been the intended target. But she'd bet her bottom dollar poor Gerr had simply been in the wrong place at the wrong time. And the wrong place and time had been with her.

Which brought her back to the question of who'd been shooting at her.

The idea it had been Liz Jermain didn't seem likely. But on the other hand, a contract killing at the resort hadn't been a likely happening, either. Nor had her being accosted in the hall. Or Harlan's appearing on her balcony in his sleep.

All in all, the highly improbable seemed to be the norm at Bride's Bay, so it made sense to ask a few questions about Liz. And that had to be what Cade was doing right now. She looked at him again, and just as she did he turned away from the concierge and started across the lobby.

"Get anywhere?" she asked when he reached her.

"Uh-uh. Nowhere at all."

"So what do we do now?"

When Cade suggested trying the bartender, they headed for the bar. There, Desmond Curtis greeted them with a warm smile. "What can I get for you two tonight? A beer and a mint julep?"

"Actually," Cade told him, "we'd just like to ask you about something. Yesterday you were telling me you've spent most of your life on the island."

"Uh-huh."

"So you must know everyone."

"Most everyone. Everyone at Bride's Bay of course. And the villagers. But a few people don't have much to do with the resort staff."

"You mean some of the people who live in the estates?" Talia said.

"That's right. Some of them keep entirely to themselves."

"We were just hearing about an old Colonel who lives there," Cade said.

"Well, him I know fairly well. He used to be concerned about the turtles," Desmond went on. "So every summer he'd ask us all to help patrol the beach when the eggs were hatching."

"He *used* to be concerned?" Cade said.

"Well, for the past year or two he...hasn't quite been himself."

Cade nodded. "That's what Liz Jermain was saying. She's the one who told us about him—we were just out walking and she gave us a ride back to the hotel. She didn't mention where she'd been, though."

"I guess," Talia tried when Desmond didn't bite, "Liz must have friends in the estates."

Her words brought the trace of a smile to the bartender's face. "Liz knows everyone on the island," he said. "But she has friends from the mainland, too."

"Yes, I imagine she would. But she wasn't visiting any of them tonight. I mean, as Cade said, she was right here—gave us a ride back to the hotel."

Desmond glanced around the almost empty bar, then looked at Talia again. "Tell me," he said quietly. "Did you hear a helicopter taking off before Liz picked you up?"

"Ah..." She and Cade had noticed a helicopter pad yesterday, when they'd walked up from the ferry, but what did a helicopter have to do with Liz's giving them a ride?

"I wasn't aware of hearing one," she finally said. "Why?"

"Oh, your question about Liz's friends just made me wonder. Because she has a friend we're all very curious about. And he sometimes comes and goes by helicopter."

"Who is he?" Cade asked.

Desmond chuckled. "If we knew that, Mr. Hailey, we wouldn't be so curious about him."

Chapter Eleven

The only thing talking to Desmond Curtis had done, Cade decided as he and Talia left the bar, was raise his frustration level.

Considering the number of detective novels he'd read in his life, he should have *some* clue about what was going on. But here he was with a real-life mystery unfolding under his nose and no idea how the pieces added up.

All he was sure of was that too many bizarre things had happened to chalk them up to coincidence. Which meant somebody was definitely targeting Talia. And knowing that made him stone cold inside.

"At least," she said as they reached the lobby, "we can be pretty certain it wasn't Liz doing the shooting."

"Yeah. I guess that was a crazy thought in the first place. It's a lot easier to believe she has a secret lover than that she moonlights as a killer."

The tiny smile Talia gave him made him want to take her in his arms.

"Cade?" She stopped walking as they reached one of the couches in the lobby. "Could we sit down for a minute? Try to see if we can figure out any of this before we go upstairs?"

He nodded. They *had* to figure things out, because he just couldn't let anything more happen to her. Maybe he didn't know who was out to get her, but he knew how he felt about her. He loved her. And he was going to do everything possible to keep her from harm.

"What about this Colonel?" she asked, sinking onto the couch. "Do you think it's possible Liz was right? Could it have been him?"

"I don't know," he said, sitting down beside her. "If he's got both a wife and a nurse keeping a close watch on him, it sure doesn't seem likely."

She nodded slowly. "And even if he'd gotten out of his house and walked along the road, he'd have to be blind to think Gerr and I were raccoons. And if he was blind," she added with another wan smile, "he couldn't have come so close to hitting us."

Cade managed to laugh, but it took a lot of effort. There was absolutely nothing humorous about all this. "But if we scratch the Colonel as a possibility," he said, "where does that leave us?"

"Lord only knows. Maybe..."

When she stopped midsentence, Cade followed her gaze across the lobby and saw that Liz and the Judge were heading in their direction. By the time they reached the couch they were both smiling, but the smiles looked strained.

"Here you are," Liz said. "When there was no answer in either of your rooms, we wondered if we'd be able to find you. But we wanted to let you know the Judge spoke to the Colonel's wife."

"Yes," he said. "We had a lengthy chat."

"And?" Cade prompted.

"And according to her, it couldn't have been the Colonel out there. He always sleeps from after dinner until about midnight. After that, he gets up and wanders around the house for hours. But until midnight, he's out like a light."

"There's no chance he broke his pattern tonight?" Talia asked.

"I don't think so. Apparently either his wife or the nurse look in on him every half hour when he's sleeping. And they've had special locks installed so he can't slip outside without them knowing."

"She also said," Liz put in, "there's no way he could've gotten hold of a gun—short of breaking in somewhere and stealing one. She got rid of his guns long ago."

"Well," Talia murmured, "we didn't really think it could have been him, but..." She paused, slowly shaking her head, and when she finally went on she sounded incredibly weary. "We're not going to find out who it was, are we? It's like last night, like the guy in the hall. We're just not going to find out who it was."

Cade covered her hand with his, wishing he could do a lot more than that to reassure her.

"Well," the Judge said, "some of the other islanders have been known to shoot at raccoons, so even if it wasn't the Colonel..."

"No," Talia said. "That can't explain it. I might have believed your senile Colonel thought he saw a coon on the beach, but..." She didn't have to finish the thought. The others nodded.

"Don't you think we should inform the sheriff's people?" Cade asked after a moment.

"Actually," the Judge said, "I've already called them."

"And?"

When the Judge glanced at Liz, she explained.

"The way they see it," she said, "all that happened was somebody shot off a few rounds out in the middle of nowhere. So they said there's no need for alarm."

"They implied," the Judge muttered, "that I was overreacting. That I was spooked because of the murder."

"And since nobody was hurt," Liz went on, "there's no way they're coming all the way over to the island this late."

"I couldn't get hold of the sheriff himself," the Judge said, "but I should be able to tomorrow. In the meantime, Talia, if it would make you feel better we could post someone from security outside your door."

"Oh, I...I just don't know. Let me think about it, all right?"

"Of course." He dug into his pocket and produced a card. "I'll write Liz's number on here, too. And if you decide you'd like someone, just call one of us."

"I will. And thanks."

As Liz and the Judge headed away Talia turned to Cade. "You know what I think? I think the guy out there was my weirdo. And maybe this is going to sound pretty crazy, but I don't want them sending somebody to stand guard outside my door. Because the way things are going, it would turn out to be him. I mean, have you noticed there's never anyone from security on the scene when there's trouble?"

Cade hesitated. Thinking the weirdo might be someone on staff *did* sound pretty crazy. At a place like this, potential employees were probably scrutinized within an inch of their lives before they were hired. But Talia was so upset he sure didn't want to say the wrong thing.

"I guess," he said at last, "we can't be too careful when there aren't many people we can definitely rule out. I mean, there's Roger, because there was no smell of cordite."

"And Gerr," Talia said, "because he was with me. But beyond that..."

A flash of realization struck Cade. "Oh, my God," he said. "Talia, I know who our weirdo is—for sure this time."

"READY TO FACE HIM if he's in there?" Cade asked as they started down the hall.

Talia nodded, but she didn't look very certain. Before they'd come upstairs, she'd said that she'd somehow developed a feeling Harlan *wasn't* their weirdo. So now that the pieces of the puzzle were finally coming together, it was clear she didn't like the picture they were forming.

"But you'll keep in mind," she said, "there could be another explanation. After all, we were wrong about Harlan last night. It wasn't him in the hall."

"We don't know that for sure. We only know he claims it wasn't."

"Yes, that's true. But I just have this feeling..."

"Look, Talia, an hour ago somebody was shooting at you. And Harlan said he keeps a gun at his motel. So it's hardly a major leap to conclude he can use one."

"But so can a zillion other people."

"True. But a zillion other people didn't tell me they weren't leaving their room till morning, then went out."

"Maybe he didn't go out. Maybe when Liz called looking for us, he was in the shower or something."

"He had a shower before dinner. He's not *that* much of a clean freak."

"Okay...but maybe something unexpected came up. So just promise you won't do anything rash."

They'd reached his room, so he merely nodded. Then he unlocked the door and shoved it open, telling himself that if Harlan was there he'd count to a hundred before saying a word. But his resolve vanished the second he saw his roommate.

When he'd left earlier Harlan had been wearing his kung fu pajamas. Now he was sitting on his bed wearing jeans, a sweatshirt and such a guilty expression even a saint would have lost his temper.

"Okay, Harlan," he snapped, slamming the door shut. "Turn off the damn TV and let's hear what the story is."

Harlan's glance flickered nervously to Talia, then back to Cade. "What's got you going this time?"

"We know you were out there shooting at Talia, so what's the deal?"

"Out there shooting at Talia?" Harlan fumbled for the remote and clicked off a weatherman midsentence.

"Harlan, you're about three seconds away from getting pitched off the balcony, so let's hear the truth."

"Cade, I don't know what you're talking about! I swear I don't. I haven't been anywhere. I—"

"Oh? You've been sitting right here all night, have you? You only changed out of your pajamas in case somebody came to visit?"

Harlan brushed his hand down his sweatshirt, looking like a kid caught with his hand in the cookie jar. Without even being aware of moving, Cade started forward, then was abruptly jerked to a stop. Talia had a death grip on his arm.

"Harlan," she said, "you did go out, didn't you."

"Well…" He rubbed his palms on his jeans. "Yeah, okay, I went out. But I only went for a walk. I had something to think about. Needed to clear my head."

"Then why lie?" Cade said. "Why tell us you were in here all night when you weren't?"

"Because I didn't want you asking what I had to think about! Because I haven't figured out what I should do about it yet. But I sure as hell wasn't shooting at Talia."

"Okay, okay," she said quietly. "But if you were out, did you at least hear the shots?"

"No." He shook his head and wiped a trickle of sweat from his forehead.

"Which way did you walk?" she pressed.

"Just along the shore. Down to that old lighthouse at the end of the island."

The opposite direction from the way Talia and Gerr had been walking, Cade realized. But Harlan's saying he'd gone down to the lighthouse didn't mean it was true. Hell, he'd started off saying he hadn't been out at all, so how could they believe anything he told them?

"You can ask that old bell captain," Harlan muttered. "He'll tell you where I was. I ran into him near the lighthouse. He says he walks down there most nights."

"Shadroe Teach?" Talia said.

"Yeah, that's what he said his name was."

"How long ago did you see him there?" Cade demanded.

"I don't know exactly. I got back fifteen or twenty minutes ago, and we were talking for quite a while. Well, mostly he was talking."

"So you were with him about an hour ago?" Talia asked.

Harlan nodded.

"Cade?" she said quietly.

"I know," he muttered. The island was roughly five miles long. So if Harlan had been at the far end of it at the approximate time of the shooting he obviously wasn't their man. But had he really been there?

"Talk to Shadroe Teach in the morning," Harlan said, glaring over at them. "He'll tell you he saw me." With that, he shoved himself off the bed and stomped into the bathroom, slamming the door for emphasis.

Cade looked at Talia, half expecting her to say she'd told him there could be another explanation.

She didn't say a word, though. And since he couldn't think of anything to say, either, he just shrugged. But dammit, if Harlan was telling the truth they were back to square one again.

EVENTUALLY HARLAN MARCHED out of the bathroom and settled himself on his bed once more, still so obviously angry that Talia, sitting on the love seat with Cade, could feel the negative vibes in the air.

She cleared her throat unhappily. Nobody would claim to have an eyewitness if he didn't, so Harlan's story had to be true. Which meant an apology was definitely in order.

But Harlan hardly looked in a receptive mood. He'd switched on the television again without so much as a glance at her and Cade.

"Harlan?" she said.

He graced her with a silent glare.

"Harlan, I'm sorry. Cade and I are both really sorry. It was just . . . oh, you can't imagine how scary it is to get shot at. And not knowing who it was . . ."

"So not knowing, you assumed it was me," he snapped "Just like last night. You two really have it in for me, don't you? Look, I know you must be scared, but I'm getting sick of you jumping down my throat every time something happens. Instead of keeping it up, why don't you figure out which of the other jurors might be trying to kill you?"

She simply stared at him while his words sank in. "What," she finally whispered, "makes you think it's one of the other jurors?"

"Nothing," he said so quickly she knew he was lying again.

"Dammit, Harlan," Cade said, "stop playing games and tell us what you know."

"I'm not sure I should. I found out something that . . . It's why I went out, what I had to think about. But I still couldn't decide whether—"

"What?" Cade practically shouted. "What the hell did you find out?"

Instead of answering, Harlan studied the tops of his sneakers. He could only do that for so long, though. And whatever he knew, Talia wasn't leaving this room until she knew it, too. She'd wait for hours if that was how long it took him to talk.

But she could tell Cade wasn't as willing to let the silence work for them this time around, which meant that trying to coax Harlan along a little was a wise idea. "Harlan," she said, "whatever you learned obviously has to do with what's been happening to me. So please tell us what it is."

He shrugged. "I could get in real trouble."

"Look," Cade said, "how about if Talia and I promise not to repeat anything you tell us? Only the three of us will ever know about it."

Harlan glanced at Talia. "You'll go along with that? You'll give me your word?"

"Cross my heart, Harlan."

"Well . . ." he began, then paused.

She held her breath, willing him to continue.

"Okay," he finally muttered. "But nobody except the three of us ever hears any of this, right?"

"Right," she and Cade agreed.

"Okay, then. Remember when you went down to the bar after dinner?" he asked Cade. "Remember I said I was going to connect with my buddy in Arizona?"

"Uh-huh." Cade glanced at Talia. "He means on his computer." She nodded.

"Well, when I got hold of him," Harlan continued, "the first thing he said was, 'Hey, is any of that stuff about your deliberations right?'"

"Meaning?" Cade asked.

"Meaning," Harlan said, "stuff about our day's deliberations showed up on the systems."

"What do you mean, stuff?" Cade asked.

"You mean on the Internet?" Talia said at the same time.

"Systems," Harlan said, apparently deciding to field her question first, "refers to any of the systems with gateways to the Internet—Prodigy, America Online, CompuServe, et cetera, et cetera. You pick any one of them and we're on it."

"*What's* on it?" Cade demanded.

"I told you. Stuff about the day's deliberations."

"You mean rumors? Speculation?"

"No. I mean cold hard facts. Right down to word-for-word quotes of what people said in that conference room. Right down to there being no doubt that Talia voted guilty on the initial ballot."

"How can that be possible?" she asked.

"Well, you made it pretty obvious from things you said today."

"I think what she meant," Cade said, "is how did the information get out?"

Harlan shrugged. "That's exactly what I wanted to know. So I started searching for an explanation. Which is what could land me in trouble. Going into all the BBS stuff, I mean."

"BBS stuff?" Talia repeated.

"Bulletin-board systems stuff," he explained. "That's like listening to what people are saying about the trial and reading papers and everything they told us not to do." He glanced at the door as if he expected a SWAT team to come bursting in at any second.

"Harlan, you wouldn't get into *that* much trouble," Cade told him.

"Says you," he muttered.

"We promised we wouldn't tell anyone," Talia quickly reminded him, in case he was having second thoughts about confiding in them.

"Well," he finally said, "okay, then. Whenever there's a halfway interesting murder trial anywhere, there are always discussion groups. You wouldn't believe how much stuff there was when O.J. Simpson—"

"Harlan?" Cade interrupted. "How do you think quotes from *our* deliberations got plastered all over the place?"

Harlan shrugged again. "Well, at first I thought we had another computer junkie on the jury, that he'd anonymously posted stuff to a news group, and it had spread."

Talia almost groaned. All she wanted to know was who was trying to kill her, but it was taking Harlan forever to get to the point.

"I wondered why somebody who was into computer networking hadn't mentioned it to me," he went on. "But I figured that had to be what the story was. Because for a computer type, posting news that nobody else knows is a big deal."

"Yes, I understand," Talia said as patiently as she could.

"So I was sure one of the other jurors was getting his kicks posting the stuff—even though he knew he wasn't supposed to."

"Why were you sure it had to be a juror?" Cade asked. "Couldn't it have been someone who just made a few lucky guesses? Or hell, maybe the conference room's bugged. At this stage nothing would surprise me."

Harlan shook his head. "I thought of a bug, too, but that's not it. Like I said, some of the stuff was real specific—exactly who said what. And with eleven men's voices, you could never be sure of all the identities on a tape. It had to be somebody right in the room."

"But who?" Talia asked, her stomach doing flip-flops. "And why?"

"I don't know who. I'm pretty sure of why, though. See, I started trying to find the original posting, but no matter what boards I checked, the news was second-hand. Then I finally got to the bottom of things and discovered why."

"Why?" Cade prompted.

Harlan paused, glancing uneasily at Talia. "Well, see, it's like I said at the start. If somebody's really trying to kill you it might be one of the jury. Because the original stuff wasn't posted to any news group, after all. It was sent to Joey Carpaccio."

Chapter Twelve

While Harlan was explaining how he'd worked his way through the maze of bulletin boards and showing them the information he'd printed out, Cade concentrated so hard his head hurt. But at least he had the story straight by the time Harlan was winding down.

Joey Carpaccio had an informer on the jury. A mole. And all the information on the systems had originally come from an electronic mail message he'd sent to Carpaccio—or more precisely to Carpaccio's people—telling them about the day's deliberations.

It had ended up on the bulletin boards after some computer hacker, who called himself Houdini, had intercepted and read the E-mail. Actually he'd decoded it first, because the original had been encoded for security. Then he'd posted it for the whole world to see. As Harlan had explained, computer types got a big kick out of posting news nobody else knew.

Cade wasn't clear on how somebody could break into an E-mail system, but Harlan claimed that everyone knew you couldn't rely on their security. And that an ingenious hacker could do just about anything.

At any rate, the how wasn't important. The important thing was that a leak from a juror, at this stage of the game, could only result in a mistrial. And even though that meant they'd all just wasted six weeks of their lives, at least they'd be getting out of here.

Thinking about that made Cade feel as if he'd been in free-fall and had just spotted a safety net. As soon as the jurors were excused, Joey Carpaccio would have nothing to gain from killing Talia.

He looked at her sitting beside him on the love seat and told himself the past six weeks really hadn't been a waste at all. In fact, they just might have been the most important weeks of his life, because if it hadn't been for this trial he'd never have met her.

"So, that's pretty much it," Harlan concluded as Cade tuned back in to what he was saying.

"Amazing," he said. "But in everything you saw, there was no clue about which juror is working for Carpaccio?"

Harlan shook his head.

"And there's absolutely no way of figuring it out?" Talia asked.

Cade was curious to hear Harlan's answer. Even though their jury wouldn't exist much longer, he'd sure like to know who was the snake in the grass. And he'd like the guy to get what he deserved.

"Actually," Harlan said, "I already tried to figure out who it is. I checked the calls that were made from the hotel today to see if any were to computer-system numbers.''

"You checked the calls?" Cade repeated. "You mean you got the desk to hand over that kind of information?"

"Well…no. But the software they're using here isn't real tough to infiltrate, so I kind of broke into their records. Right from our room here."

"Isn't that illegal?" Cade said.

Harlan shrugged, looking only marginally guilty. "I decided it was okay under the circumstances. But I didn't find out anything useful. The only calls that would have gotten anyone onto the information highway were mine."

"Then how did our mole send his E-mail?"

"He must have a cell phone. And a laptop that can interface with one. That way he wouldn't have had to use the hotel lines."

"He certainly came prepared, didn't he," Cade muttered. "And if there's no phone record, then there's just no possible way of finding out who he is?"

"If I knew which system he used, and could get into its log, I'd have a chance. But that's a whole different ball game than breaking into the hotel records."

The three of them sat in silence until Cade finally said, "Well, maybe we'll never know who the mole is, but at least everything's going to be okay now. Just as soon as—"

"I don't think you should get overconfident," Harlan interrupted. "After all, at this point Joey's certain Talia's convinced he's guilty."

"But what Joey's certain of isn't important anymore," Cade said.

"What do you mean?"

"I mean it's all over."

"Over?"

Cade nodded. "If half of what we talked about today is on those bulletin boards and thousands of people are reading it, then—"

"More like hundreds of thousands."

"Okay, so hundreds of thousands of people know that someone on this jury leaked information. And those hundreds of thousands are going to include cops and lawyers and court officials and members of the media. First thing in the morning, they'll all be blowing the whistle. Which will leave Joey Carpaccio looking at a retrial."

"Oh, no, Cade," Harlan said. "You're wrong. Nobody who's read the stuff on the bulletin boards is going to blow any whistles."

Harlan had to have known that he and Talia were waiting for him to elaborate, but he simply looked at them, his expression smug.

"All right," Cade said at last, "tell us why nobody's going to blow the whistle."

"Because bulletin boards are big grapevines, always full of rumors and gossip. Everybody knows that, so why would it even occur to anybody that the stuff about us originated from a juror?"

"But…didn't it say that someplace?" Talia asked.

Harlan shook his head. "*I* said that, because I knew it had to have come from somebody in that conference room. But Houdini didn't say it. All he did was post the information. So people are going to figure it's nothing more than speculation. And nobody's going to start yelling about a leak from the jury on the basis of speculation.''

Cade rubbed his jaw, considering Harlan's logic. Ridiculous as it seemed, he could see Harlan might be right.

''Cade?'' Talia said. ''If that's the situation, what do we do now?''

''What we do,'' he said firmly, ''is blow the whistle ourselves. We'll have to talk to Bud and tell him everything. And we may as well do it right now. I guess he won't be able to report it till the morning, but—''

''No!'' Harlan objected. ''You gave me your word you wouldn't say anything. I'll get in trouble if you do.''

''Dammit, Harlan, you're not going to get into any *serious* trouble. And it was a blind promise. There are limits to blind promises.''

''Not in my books there aren't! And if you blow your stupid whistle the mole will get away with what he did. They'll never figure out who he is.''

''Maybe they won't. But Talia won't get killed, either. As soon as Bud reports what's happened we'll be on our way home and she'll be safe.''

''No,'' Harlan said again. ''Nobody should help a guy like Joey Carpaccio and not get caught. I...I wasn't going to say, but I'm the other one who voted guilty. All three of us know that creep paid somebody to kill his wife. And now he's got somebody trying to murder Talia, too. You don't want him to get away with trying to kill you, do you Talia? It just wouldn't be right."

"Harlan," she said quietly, "I agree with you. It wouldn't be right. But there really doesn't seem to be anything we can do about it."

"Yes, there is. I can figure out who the mole is."

"I thought you just told us you couldn't," Cade said.

"Well . . . I didn't want to say I could, because the only way would be if somebody else helps me out. And I don't know if they would or not."

"But if they did?" Talia said. "Then you *could* figure it out?"

"Maybe. But I'd need some time."

"Harlan," Cade said, "as you just finished pointing out, Joey's got somebody trying to murder Talia. Given that, we hardly want to prolong things."

"I wouldn't need *much* time."

"How much?" Talia asked.

"Look," Cade muttered, "it doesn't matter how much."

"No, wait," she said slowly. "Let's just think about this for a minute. Harlan has a good point. I don't want Joey Carpaccio to get away with trying to have me killed. And if Bud won't be able to report the leak until the morning, anyway . . ."

"Right," Harlan jumped in. "And if I start right now, maybe by morning I'll have something. And if I could tell the cops who the mole is, then I probably wouldn't be in any trouble at all. And they'd be able to get everything they need to know out of him. They'd be able to charge Carpaccio with jury tampering or whatever. And find out who was shooting at you."

Talia glanced from Harlan to Cade. "But I just assumed . . . it was the mole shooting at me, wasn't it? I mean, if he's working for Joey . . ."

She looked so upset Cade reached for her hand. "I don't think the mole and your shooter are necessarily the same person," he said quietly. "Do you, Harlan?"

He shook his head. "They could be. But they don't have to be. Joey Carpaccio could easily have more than one guy on his payroll."

"Joey Carpaccio," Cade muttered, "could easily have ten guys on his payroll."

"Ten?" Talia whispered.

"Sorry." He squeezed her hand. "I didn't mean to make things sound even worse than they are. And I was exaggerating. This island is a close little community, so he couldn't send ten goons over here without people realizing something awfully strange was going on. But he might have sent one guy. The mole's only job might be supplying information."

"Or he might be doing more," Harlan said.

Cade nodded. "One guy, two guys, we just don't have any way of knowing, do we?"

INSTEAD OF USING the connecting door, Cade led Talia into the hallway. At her door, he kept right on walking, Talia's hand still firmly in his.

"I thought you were just walking me to my room," she said, hurrying to keep up with him.

"I only said that for Harlan's benefit. There's something I want to do, and I'm not leaving you alone."

"Well, I could've stayed with him."

"Uh-uh."

"Why not?"

Cade merely gave her a sidelong glance.

"Why not?" she repeated as they started down the stairs. She didn't want him keeping anything from her. She was undoubtedly going to remain scared half to death until this was over, anyway, so she'd just as soon know the worst.

"Something struck me," he said at last. "About two seconds after you and Harlan convinced me to go along with giving him until morning."

"And the something is?"

"Talia, it's just possible *Harlan's* the mole."

"What? Oh, Cade, you're being absurd."

"Not necessarily. The way he was talking, he made it sound as if the three of us are in this together. But think about the facts. Harlan knows all about E-mail. He could just as easily have a cell phone in his suitcase as any of the other jurors. And we don't know for sure where he was when that guy stuck a gun in your back last night—it still could have been him. And tonight... well, who's to say he wasn't lying about being at that lighthouse with Shadroe Teach, thinking we'd just believe him without bothering to check?"

"I doubt he'd be dumb enough to think that."

"No?" They reached the lobby and started across it. "Well, we're not taking any chances, so we're going to ask Teach right now."

"It's awfully late to disturb him."

"I know. But our friendly bartender told me he and Teach go way back, so I thought he might do the disturbing for us. And if Teach didn't see Harlan tonight, we won't be giving him a few seconds, never mind a few hours. We'll be going straight to Bud. And we'll be calling the cops again, too—whether they like having to come over to the island in the middle of the night or not."

"All right," Talia said. There was no point in disagreeing when Cade's mind was obviously made up. And if Harlan *had* lied to them . . .

He hadn't, though. Not about talking to Shad Teach. She was sure of that.

"All right," she said again. "But I don't think there's even a chance Harlan's the mole, because it makes no sense. If he was, why on earth would he have told us about everything being on those bulletin boards? Why wouldn't he have just kept quiet?"

"Because the best defense is a good offense."

"Which means?"

"Which means that when he discovered his secret message had ended up all over the place he had a choice. Either he could just pray nobody would find out what he'd done, or he could try to cover up—by dragging us into things and painting himself as completely innocent. Hell, even telling us he was the other one who voted guilty could have been a crock."

She started to reply, then stopped herself. She didn't know what to say. Because even though she really didn't believe Harlan was their man, she had to admit it was a possibility.

As they reached the bar, that possibility started a chilly little sense of apprehensiveness worming around inside her. *Had* they just aligned themselves with the enemy?

Cade settled her into a wing chair that clearly wasn't a random choice. Its back was against a wall, it wasn't anywhere near a window, and it was only about ten feet from where Desmond Curtis was standing behind the bar.

"Look," Cade said, gazing down at her, his gray eyes full of concern, "I'd like to see the mole caught as much as you would. And if there's another guy involved I'd like him to get nailed, too. But I'm more concerned about your safety than about anything else."

"I'm pretty concerned about it, too," she murmured.

"Good." He gave her a warm smile. "Then let's just keep our priorities straight. And don't move out of this chair, okay? I'll only be a minute."

She watched him cross to the bar and start talking to Desmond, wondering how she could feel so totally wired and so incredibly tired at the same time. But it wasn't really surprising. She hadn't gotten a minute's sleep last night. And almost getting killed would put *most* people on edge.

At the bar, Desmond had already picked up a phone. He spoke for a minute or two, then hung up and said something to Cade.

Cade nodded, then turned and strode back over to her. "Harlan's alibi checked out," he said, sending a rush of relief through her. At least whoever had been shooting at her wasn't sleeping in the bed beside Cade's. And in the room next to hers.

Without saying another word, Cade returned to the bar, and began talking to Desmond again. Briefly she wondered what he was saying, then her thoughts drifted back to Harlan.

He wasn't their shooter, but that didn't guarantee he wasn't the mole. Cade's theory that he might be didn't seem likely, but unlikely and impossible were two different things. And if Harlan *was* working for Carpaccio...

Harlan had said there was virtually no way of figuring out who'd sent that E-mail, but what if that wasn't true?

What if he'd lied, trying to buy time? Maybe enough time for somebody to succeed at getting rid of her? And maybe get rid of Cade, too, now that he knew too much?

The thoughts were enough to make her shiver. And make her decide that the next time somebody asked her to give them a little time, they'd probably get a flat-out no.

If there ever was a next time. For anything.

ON THE WAY BACK to Cade's room, Talia was still wondering what he and Desmond Curtis had been talking about. She'd asked of course, but all she'd gotten in reply was a curt "Don't worry about it."

That had annoyed her—more than a little. The only thing that kept her from pressing was knowing Cade had to be almost as edgy as she was. After all, he was hanging around with a target for murder, not exactly the safest place to be.

But at least he *was* still hanging around with her. And if it hadn't been for that she'd have melted into a pool of fear long before this, so she wasn't going to let a few curt words gnaw away at her. She forced them from her mind as he unlocked his door.

Inside the room Harlan glanced up from his laptop and looked at them with a broad grin. "Where were you guys? I knocked on the door, and you weren't in Talia's room."

"We just went down to the bar for a few minutes," Cade told him. "Why? What's up?"

"I heard from Houdini!" Harlan announced, pushing his glasses up on his nose.

For a second she drew a blank. Then she remembered that was the nickname of the hacker who'd intercepted the mole's E-mail.

"You heard from him?" Cade was saying.

"Right. *He's* who I needed help from. So I posted a message for him on the boards as soon as you left. I didn't know if he'd reply, but he did—right away. And I convinced him to send me a copy of the original message. The way it was before he decoded it, I mean.''

"And?'' Talia said. Since Harlan already had a copy of the decoded version, she had no idea why this should be a big deal. But it clearly was.

"And then I ran down to the desk and got a copy made of the pages.''

"Why,'' Cade asked.

Harlan shrugged. "I might need a clean original. But I wanted a working copy, so I can translate it myself.''

"Translate it?'' Talia said. "But if it's already decoded . . . Or does translating mean something different?''

"No, same thing. But see, the original's in some weird homemade code, not one my computer can deal with. And Houdini decoded it really fast, because all he cared about was the content. But if I take enough time to do it carefully it'll be way more precise.''

"And?'' she said again, starting to feel like a parrot.

"And there might be something in it. A clue to who sent it.''

"That's how you're going to try to figure out who our mole is?'' Cade said.

Harlan nodded. "See, Houdini wouldn't have worried about translating anything but the facts, so he might've left out something that would strike a chord with us.''

"Great,'' Cade said. "That's fantastic,'' he added, making Harlan's grin grow even broader.

Talia glanced at him curiously. He sounded awfully sincere for someone who hadn't ruled Harlan out as the mole.

"I'll tell you what," Cade continued. "Let's divide things up. While you're decoding the message, Talia and I can work our way through the list of jurors. Some of them couldn't possibly be the mole, and simple logic should let us eliminate them."

"You can begin with the three of us," Harlan suggested.

"Exactly. And if we can reduce the rest to only a few possibilities, instead of nine..."

"Okay," Harlan said, nodding happily. "Okay, let's get started."

"We'll just go into Talia's room. So our talking doesn't disturb you."

She looked at Cade again, and the way he held her gaze made her think he might have some other reason for his suggestion. Then she told herself she was wrong.

But if she was, how could there be so much warmth in his eyes?

Chapter Thirteen

"Fine, you two just go ahead," Harlan said as Talia managed to force her gaze from Cade's. "It'll take me a while to redo this message," he continued, "because it wasn't exactly a four-liner. And I want to do a good job decoding it. But at least—" he glanced at her "—you don't have to worry about me showing up on your balcony again tonight. I'm sure not going to waste any time sleeping."

"Good," Cade said. "Well, let's get going." He reached for Talia's hand and led her into her own room before she could utter another word.

She switched on the light as he locked the door, then looked at him. "Was it only my imagination," she said, "or did you suddenly decide you couldn't stand spending another ten seconds with Harlan?"

Cade laughed. It was a quiet laugh, but so deep and masculine and sexy it made her feel warm all over.

For a few seconds, she thought again about how he'd appeared from nowhere earlier, when she'd been terrified on the beach—thought back to how safe and protected he'd made her feel simply by holding her. It was one of the few times she'd felt safe lately. And it was also the moment she'd known, with absolute certainty, she was in love with him.

But he wasn't in love with her. The warm feeling faded as she recalled what he'd said. She'd asked him what he was doing there, and he'd replied, "Making sure you're okay. That's what friends are for."

Friends.

He considered her nothing more than a friend. So the look she'd seen in his eyes a few minutes ago had been simple affection. Nothing at all like what she felt for him. And knowing that made her heart ache.

"Well," she said, telling herself feelings couldn't *really* make a heart ache, "I guess we'd better get started eliminating jurors."

When she turned and headed toward the sitting area, Cade followed her. And when she sat down in the exact center of a love seat, so there wasn't room for him on either side, he sank onto the one opposite.

"So," she began, realizing her throat was aching as badly as her heart, "what do you think? If we figure out who the mole is do we solve the whole mystery? Or are the odds higher that Joey *does* have somebody else over here?" Absently she kicked off her sneakers, then noticed Cade was watching her.

She shrugged. "I think better without my shoes on."

"Really?" He kicked off his. "Maybe it'll work for me, too. And to answer your question . . . Hell, Talia, I know it's not the answer you'd like to hear, but I bet there *is* somebody else."

"That's what I think, too," she said quietly. "So we've got a juror we can't identify and a hired gun who could be just about anybody."

Cade leaned forward, making her glad there was a coffee table between the love seats. There were a whole lot of different emotions burbling inside her at the moment, which she was having a hard time keeping under control. And seeing that the warmth was back in Cade's eyes again wasn't helping. It was only making her want to believe things she knew weren't true.

"Look," he said gently, "we can still call the police right now if you want."

She shook her head. "We're safe here in this room, aren't we?"

He nodded.

"Then we should give Harlan time. Especially since Houdini cooperated with him. I mean, maybe he *will* figure out who the mole is."

"Maybe," Cade agreed, still gazing across the coffee table at her.

"But is there really any point in our sitting here trying to eliminate jurors? Especially if Joey's got two people working for him? If the real danger is from somebody we've never even heard of?"

"Maybe there isn't much point," Cade admitted. "But there didn't seem much point in sitting in the other room with Harlan, either, just watching him pore over that message."

She swallowed hard, telling herself Cade wasn't really looking at her as if he was a starving man and she was a gourmet meal. Then she ordered her imagination to stop acting up, because under the circumstances, sitting here alone with him was bad enough. But her imagination kept right on tormenting her— until a knock on the door stopped it in its tracks and started her heart pounding.

Motioning her to stay where she was, Cade answered the door, then went out into the hall to talk to whoever had knocked. Not knowing who was out there with him sent her anxiety level soaring. Then her imagination went to work again, this time insisting it was a killer who'd come calling, so she was vastly relieved when Cade stepped back inside. He closed the door and simply stood looking at her for a second.

"Well?" she said when he started back across the room without volunteering anything.

He shrugged. "Just a message for me."

"For you."

"Uh-huh."

That added up, she told herself. If somebody had gone to his room, Harlan would have sent them here. She was about to ask what the message had been when he reached the sitting area and gestured her to move over, so there'd be room for him beside her. When he sat down, the length of his thigh pressed against hers and heat from his leg began seeping into her body. It made her pulse begin a wild dance of arousal.

She took a deep breath hoping it would calm her, but all it did was make her intensely aware of his woodsy scent. And something about it was far more enticing than the smell of real woods. Far more enticing, in fact, than anything else she could think of.

Trying to ignore both her erratic pulse and the fluttering around her heart, she racked her brain for something to say. Something that would sound as if she didn't find his presence the slightest bit disturbing.

"The message," she finally said. "Who was it from?"

"Desmond Curtis. While we were downstairs I asked him about borrowing something."

"Borrowing what?"

Cade reached under his sweater and took out a gun he'd had tucked in his waistband.

She stared at it as he set it on the coffee table. It was matte black and evil-looking, but she certainly wasn't unhappy to see it.

"A Browning semiautomatic," he said. "Thirteen rounds in the magazine."

"Ah." She wasn't unhappy about that, either. Even with a limited knowledge of guns, she knew rounds were bullets.

"It belongs to a friend of Desmond's."

She nodded, her gaze still on the gun, wondering if Cade really did believe they were safe in this room. Then, without consciously thinking about it, she looked toward the dark balcony.

Cade rose, silently crossed the room and switched off the lights. Then he walked over to the French doors and stood staring out into the moonlight.

"Nothing there," he finally said, turning and starting back toward her. "And the gun is just insurance. I really do think we're okay at the moment. So why don't you try to relax?'' He sat down beside her again without turning the lights back on.

"Yes," she managed. "Relaxing would be a nice change." But it was the last thing she could do. They might be okay at the moment, but sitting in the moonlight with him was definitely not conducive to relaxing.

Her gaze met his, which reminded her that was something she should avoid. Even in only the moonlight, those warm gray eyes of his were magnetic. Or maybe it was everything about him that was magnetic. And like any magnet, the closer he got the harder it was to resist his pull.

They simply sat in silence for a minute, and then he rested his hand on her thigh. She almost turned to liquid on the spot, and when he began to trace tiny circles with his thumb things got worse. Her pulse started beating a thousand times a second, and a hundred tiny fires ignited inside her.

When she looked at his face again he was eyeing her intently. And his expression was telling her things he'd never said aloud. Things she'd give anything to hear him say.

Or maybe it was only her imagination at work again. After all, she'd misread his expressions before, had misread *him* before. In fact, she'd misread him constantly. Throughout the entire trial, she'd assumed he was falling for her—until he'd made it clear he hadn't been.

"Tomorrow's our last day together," he said quietly. "Once the jury's dismissed, everyone will go their separate ways."

She nodded, afraid to open her mouth. Afraid of what that look of desire she was imagining in his eyes might make her say. "Like ships that pass in the night," she finally risked.

"Exactly," he agreed, beginning to move his thumb slowly up and down a few inches of her thigh.

It was definitely not the caress of a friend. It was a caress that made her so hot she had to mount a major effort to keep from squirming. Then, without a word, he abruptly stood up and started across the room. For one horrible second she thought he was walking out on her again. Then she realized he wasn't heading for the door.

He reached the bed, which left him with no farther to walk, so he began pacing the floor at the end of it. She watched him, watched the way moon shadows were painting the planes and angles of his face until her fingers began to itch with wanting to trace them.

"Look," he finally said, "I know this is just about the worst timing in the history of the world, but there's not much I can do about it."

"Do about what?"

He didn't answer, simply looked at her. Even from across the room the pull between them was too strong to resist.

She rose and walked over to him. "Do about what?" she repeated softly.

He still didn't answer. He simply wrapped his arms around her and kissed her. The kiss was as gentle as spring rain, yet it sent shock waves all the way to her toes. His lips possessed. His tongue teased. His hands smoothed their way down her back, pressing every inch of her body against his.

It made nerve endings she hadn't even known existed tingle with need, and it made her intensely aware they were standing right beside the bed. Then, far too soon, he eased away a little. Only his arms, looped around her waist, maintained contact.

She gazed silently up at him, resisting the temptation to run her fingers along his chiseled jaw. She was feeling so shaky she knew it would be dangerous to attempt the slightest movement. "I thought," she whispered, "you just wanted to be friends."

"Yeah," he said, his wry smile almost making her knees give out. "That's what I thought, too. It's what I kept telling myself, at any rate."

"Why?" she asked, then managed to stop herself before she asked what utter lunacy had prompted him to do that.

He shrugged. "Because I'm an idiot."

"No...the real reason, Cade. Be honest."

"All right," he said slowly. "Because you remind me of my ex-wife."

Talia wasn't sure how long she stood simply looking at Cade and listening to the alarm bells going off in her head.

She'd finally found the man people had always told her existed. The one who made a room light up for her merely by walking into it. But now that she had, he was turning into a classic textbook case—right before her very eyes.

Was he really one of those men who repeatedly fell for the same type of woman? A type with whom, for some reason buried deep in his psyche, he could never sustain a healthy relationship?

She prayed he wasn't, but there was only one way to find out. "How do I remind you of your ex-wife?"

"Well . . . mostly because you're so gorgeous."

Mostly because she was so gorgeous? She listened to the explanation echo around in her head for a second, wanting to be sure she'd heard him right. Because that certainly didn't sound like an insurmountable psychological problem.

And the fact it didn't made her feel as if somebody had just popped the cork of a magnum of champagne and was pouring all the bubbles directly into her bloodstream. *Hold on a minute,* an imaginary voice warned her. *Make sure you've got this straight.*

Half-afraid to, she asked, "That's it? It's mostly just because you think I'm pretty, and so's she, that I remind you of her?"

"Not pretty. Gorgeous."

"Ah, well, thank you. But you're *sure* there's nothing more . . . serious?"

"Why are you making this sound unimportant when it's not?"

"Well, it isn't exactly the—"

"Dammit, Talia, it's important to me. My marriage broke up because Marilyn was screwing around on me. And a lot of the problem was her looks. Guys were constantly coming on to her, and if she hadn't looked the way she does ... Well, you're the psychologist here. You must understand what I'm saying."

She was so immensely relieved she could feel laughter building up inside her. She tried with all her might to hold it in, told herself this definitely wasn't the time for her sense of humor to surface.

Then she told herself that laughing at something someone else considered important was a terrible thing to do. And it would make Cade angry. But she just couldn't help herself.

"What?" he said, looking thoroughly annoyed. "Talia, it's not funny. What the hell kind of psychologist are you? I tell you something personal and you laugh at me? What—"

Before he could get any more upset she cradled his face between her hands, drew it down to hers and kissed him. He didn't seem very happy about that at first, so she put a little body language into it—which helped a lot.

When his body language started talking back, she waited until it was saying he'd forgotten all about being angry with her. Then she drew her lips away from his a fraction of an inch and murmured, "I'm sorry I laughed, but I wasn't laughing at you. I swear I wasn't."

He grinned at her. "It's okay. I haven't heard you laugh in almost two days, and I've missed it."

"Oh, Cade, I haven't felt like laughing in almost two days. I was thinking my sense of humor had taken off on vacation without letting me know."

"But you felt like laughing at me. I still—"

"Shh," she whispered, pressing her fingers to his lips. "I *wasn't* laughing at you. It was only that when you said I was like your wife... well, I was just so darned relieved it turned out not to be anything really serious. Because I thought you didn't like me and—"

"You thought I didn't *like* you?" He leaned closer again and began nuzzling his way down her neck, his hot moist kisses stoking the fires he'd already ignited.

"I'm absolutely insane about you," he whispered, his breath fanning the flames.

"Oh, well, I guess it wasn't exactly that I thought you didn't like me. I just didn't think you were interested. I thought—"

He covered her lips with his once more and got down to some really serious kissing. Kissing that left no doubt just how interested he was. Deep passionate kissing that made her breathless with desire.

She ran her hands under his sweater tangling her fingers in his chest hair and making him groan. He broke their kiss long enough to tug the sweater over his head. Then he pulled hers off and quickly removed her bra.

"Oh, God," he murmured cupping her breasts and grazing her nipples with his thumbs, driving her wild with his touch. "I can't believe how much time I wasted being a fool."

Before she could point out that people should always try to make up for lost time they ended up on the bed.

"You know what?" he whispered as they struggled out of the rest of their clothes.

"What?"

"If Harlan knocks on that damn door and interrupts us I don't want you telling me I can't kill him, because I'm going to."

"You know what?"

"What?"

"I'll help you."

Cade laughed—that wonderful, quiet, sexy laugh—and she laughed with him, because her heart had stopped aching and was almost bursting with happiness. She was in love with Cade and he was...well, maybe he hadn't said *love,* but he'd said he was absolutely insane about her, and that would do just fine.

Suddenly the world seemed like a whole lot better place. At least this little corner of it. They were locked away in her room, safe from evil. And she knew what Cade had said before no longer held true. Tomorrow, once the jury was dismissed, they wouldn't *all* be going their separate ways. She and Cade...

He started trailing his fingers down her naked body, which drove the rest of that thought completely out of her mind. Tomorrow didn't matter at the moment. All that mattered was here and now.

"Talia?" Cade whispered against her neck, the warmth of his breath making her shiver. "You're okay with this? You're not so worried about everything that..."

She almost started laughing again—partly because there was too much happiness inside her to contain, partly at the absurdity of his timing. They were already lying on the bed without a stitch of clothing between them. But he was so sweet to ask, even though the answer was obvious, that she simply kissed him—starting at his forehead and working her way down his face, his neck, his chest, down to his hard belly. With a groan he grabbed her by the shoulders and pulled her up to kiss her mouth once more.

"Take it easy," he whispered. "I want it to last. I want it to be good for you."

She wanted it to be good, too, but there wasn't the faintest chance it wouldn't be. The way he was fondling her breasts was making her mad with wanting him. And the throbbing ache inside her had grown so intense that if he made it last much longer she was going to die.

"Cade?"

"What?"

She tried to go on, but he'd started kissing her breasts, teasing her nipples with his tongue, and it was making her so breathless she couldn't speak.

Then he slid his hand across her stomach, down to where the throbbing was worst, and rationality began to slip away.

"Cade," she whispered desperately, her body moving against his touch, "if it doesn't last, couldn't we just start over?"

Chapter Fourteen

The first fingers of dawn poked in through the balcony's French doors and transformed Talia's hair into spun gold.

Cade lay absently stroking it, thinking he'd never been so happy. He'd be content just to lie here with her forever the way they were—half-asleep and completely in love.

Loving her all through the night, talking with her while she lay in his arms, had made him so damn...well, happy wasn't a big enough word. Not even close to what he was feeling.

By straining his brain, he finally dredged up *euphoric*. That was an improvement, although it still didn't capture the full-to-bursting feeling that had him lying here grinning idiotically.

He closed his eyes and simply breathed in her scent. As always, it brought to mind the freshness of sea air...cool sand...moonlight. And the scent of love had been added now.

He was never going to let her get out of this bed. Never going to let her shower away the scent of their night together.

"Cade?" she whispered.

"Mmm?" He could feel her smiling against his chest.

"I was right, wasn't I? Starting over worked just fine, didn't it?"

"Well, it seemed to work just fine the first three times," he teased, "but I think we'd better grab a little sleep before we try for four."

"Really? You're getting tired of me already?"

"Not tired of you, just worried you're going to kill me."

She laughed quietly, but began to move provocatively against him. And even though he was aching, he felt a fresh stirring of arousal. He lazily caressed her breast, loving the tiny moan of pleasure she gave him in response.

"I guess an hour or two of sleep wouldn't be a bad idea," she finally whispered. "If you ended up dead in my bed people would talk."

"I think that's a good point." Cuddling her against him, he went back to stroking her hair. But the words *kill* and *dead* lingered in his thoughts, and reality began intruding on their perfection.

Reality wasn't going to allow them to stay right here forever. But even though he was going to have to let her out of this bed, he wasn't letting her out of his sight. Not until after the jury was dismissed and they were safely off Jermain Island.

Hell, he might not let her out of his sight even after they were back in Charleston. He might just stick to her like glue for the rest of his life.

Sometime during the night thoughts of marriage had begun drifting through his mind. And he felt certain that if he and Talia married it would be the forever kind of thing.

They'd talked a little about his ex-wife. And the more they'd talked, the more convinced he'd grown that Talia was nothing like Marilyn when it came to men. Talia was a one-man woman. And from now on he'd be doing everything possible to be that man.

He glanced at the clock radio, saw it wasn't yet six and wondered if Harlan had learned anything from his decoding. Probably not, he decided. In fact, definitely not. If he had, he'd have been banging on the door.

"What are you thinking about?" Talia murmured.

"Harlan."

"You were supposed to say me," she said, giving him a tiny poke in the ribs.

"Okay, it was you. In a way at least. I was thinking how glad I was Harlan didn't interrupt us during the night."

That made her laugh again, and her laugh made him smile. She had the greatest laugh in the world. "The truth is," she told him, "you were wondering if Harlan got that message translated, weren't you? And if he found the clue he was looking for."

"Yeah, I was. But I'm sure he didn't. If he'd come up with anything, he'd have interrupted."

"You don't think . . ."

"What?"

She shrugged. "If he did figure things out, you don't think he might try something on his own, do you?"

"No, he thinks the three of us are in this together, remember?"

"Maybe. But I doubt he's entirely sure he should trust us. He kept holding things back last night."

"What things? We know everything, don't we?"

"Well, enough I guess. But remember how, at first, he said there was no way he could figure out who the mole was? Then he admitted there might be. And even then, he didn't really tell us any details until after he'd heard from Houdini."

"Yeah, I see what you're getting at. So maybe I'd better check on what's happening." Reluctantly Cade rolled out of bed, pulled on his clothes, then unlocked the connecting door.

When he walked into the other room, Harlan was curled up asleep on his bed. He was fully dressed, sneakers and all, and his laptop was still on. There was no data on the screen, though.

Curiously Cade clicked the mouse to bring up what Harlan had been working on.

NO CLUE! NO CLUE! NO CLUE! appeared, followed by DAMN! DAMN! DAMN!

He stood staring at the screen for a minute, thinking how disappointed Harlan must have been at not finding anything. Then he grabbed some clean clothes, scribbled a note and went back into Talia's room.

She propped herself on one elbow and looked at him. The sheet was demurely pulled up around her bare shoulders, but he had no trouble visualizing what was beneath it.

"Well?" she finally said.

"Well, Harlan's asleep and he didn't figure out who the mole is."

"If he's asleep how do you know?"

"I snooped on his computer," he told her, tossing his clean clothes onto one of the love seats. "Then I left a note saying we were going out for a morning walk. That we'd meet him back here about eight-thirty so we could all go talk to Bud."

"A walk?" she said nervously. "You mean like on the beach? Where people have been known to get shot at?"

"That's what I said in the note." Cade tugged off his sweatshirt. "I didn't say it was the truth." He unsnapped his jeans.

TALIA POURED herself another cup of coffee, glad Cade had suggested they have breakfast in the room. Even before he'd ended up back in bed with her, she hadn't wanted to spend any more time than necessary surrounded by other people. She wanted every possible minute alone with him.

When she smiled across the table at him he said, "Happy?"

"Extremely."

"Well, you'll be a lot happier once we get out of here."

She nodded, although in the bright morning light things really didn't seem half as scary as they had last night. Oh, she still didn't intend to take any chances. But Cade had a gun now, and he'd assured her his cop uncle had taught him to shoot well.

So she'd acquired her own armed bodyguard, and she certainly wasn't going anywhere without him. Even *with* him, the only place she'd be going was to talk to Bud.

"Should we check in with Harlan?" she said, glancing across the table again.

Cade looked at his watch. "He's probably in the dining room. And my note said we'd see him at eight-thirty, so I'm sure he'll be here by then."

"Or sooner," she said as someone knocked on the door.

"Talia?" the someone called. "You in there? It's me, Gerr."

"What's *he* doing here?" Cade muttered.

She shrugged and headed for the door, checking the peephole just to make sure it really was Gerr. It was, although instead of yesterday's sophisticated look, he was dressed in Western attire today—checked shirt, jeans and cowboy boots. When she opened the door, he looked curiously past her at Cade—then at the bed they'd torn apart with their lovemaking.

"I was watching for you in the dining room," he finally said, looking at her again. "And when you didn't come in, I thought I'd try up here."

"Yes . . . well," she mumbled, her face hot, "Cade and I had something to talk about, so we thought we'd get together for breakfast and just have it in here."

"Uh, sorry to interrupt then, but can I come in for a minute?"

Stepping back, she glanced at Cade. He was eyeing Gerr with a decidedly hostile expression.

"I brought you something else you'll probably want to talk about." Gerr shoved the door closed, then held out the denim jacket he'd been carrying over his arm. "Either of you ever see this before?"

Cade shrugged. "There are an awful lot of denim jackets in the world."

"Yes, but I found this particular one hidden behind a bush near the road to town. I decided I'd just take a walk in that direction first thing this morning, to see if there were footprints or anything. And the jacket was right about where our guy would've been standing last night. There was a pair of leather gloves, too."

Cade walked over and reached for the jacket. He looked at the label, then at Gerr. "Size forty-two. That'd be about right, wouldn't it. And now that I think about it, Roger *does* have a jacket like this. He wore it on the ferry on the trip over here. Remember, Talia?"

"Yes, but are you two saying Roger was our shooter, after all?"

"Does an alligator live in the swamp?" Gerr said.

She glanced at him, thinking for a tiny second that seemed like a strange saying for a New Yorker. Then she went back to thinking about Roger.

"But last night," she said, "you both agreed there'd be a smell of gunpowder on his hands if... Oh, my Lord. That's where the gloves come in."

"Bingo," Gerr said. "And the jacket would have protected his sweater from traces of cordite. There's no smell on it now, but there sure could've been last night."

While Gerr was talking, Cade wrapped his arm around Talia's shoulders—just as well, given the sudden dizziness she was feeling.

Roger was working for Joey Carpaccio. Roger was their informer. And the shooter, too, so it looked as if she and Cade had been wrong. Joey probably didn't have two people on the island. Roger had been doing double duty.

She almost said so to Cade, then realized she shouldn't. Gerr didn't know about the mole. Or about anything else to do with the jury, for that matter. And until Bud and their trial judge—not to mention the sheriff's department and whoever else might be involved—got everything sorted out, she and Cade probably shouldn't be saying much to anyone.

"You okay?" Cade asked, giving her shoulders a little squeeze.

She nodded, but it was a lie. As much as she'd wanted to know who'd been shooting at her, finding out didn't make her feel any better. After spending six weeks with the other jurors, the fact that one of them could turn around and try to kill her made her feel downright ill.

Cade gave her another concerned glance, then looked at Gerr. "What made you go have a look? Just a hunch?"

"Not exactly. Remember after Liz drove us back last night? How when we got out of the van Roger wanted to talk to me?"

Talia and Cade nodded.

"What he wanted was to make sure I didn't think he could've done the shooting."

"But he knew that," Talia said. "I mean, he pointed out there was no smell of gunpowder. And you and Cade both agreed it couldn't have been him."

"Right. I'd already said I knew it wasn't him, but there he was, trying to convince me. And that got me wondering why he hadn't just let it drop. That's the writer's mind at work. We're always thinking about motivations. At any rate, that's why I thought I'd have a look-see.

"But now I'm wondering about something else," he went on. "Roger doesn't know me from Adam. So it had to be you he was shooting at, Talia. You know why?"

She glanced anxiously at Cade. She knew she couldn't say that Joey Carpaccio had one of the jurors in his pocket, but she didn't have a cover story on the tip of her tongue.

"The answer," Cade said, bailing her out, "is pretty straightforward. It isn't obvious when you first meet him, but our friend Roger is kind of unbalanced."

"Really?" Gerr put so much interest into the one word that Talia was certain his next book would feature an unbalanced juror.

"I wonder if he went back to get the jacket this morning," Talia said, trying to do her part by changing the subject. "After you already had it, I mean. I wonder if he figures somebody's on to him."

"I don't know," Gerr said. "But maybe the more important question is what we're going to do now that we know it was him. I guess we should call the cops, huh?"

Talia glanced at Cade again. The obvious thing to do was just tell Bud the whole story and let him call all the authorities.

The look Cade gave her said that was what he was thinking, too. Then he made an almost imperceptible gesture with his thumb, suggesting the best thing they could do was try to get rid of Gerr.

Before they had a chance, though, there was another knock on the door.

THIS TIME Cade played doorman. And this time it *was* Harlan.

"Who's that?" Harlan hissed, peering in at Gerald Asimov. "And what's he doing in there? I need to talk to you two."

Cade stepped out into the hall and pulled the door almost shut. "That's the lawyer-writer I told you about last night. The guy Talia had dinner with. And he just showed up.''

"But I need to talk to you," Harlan said again. "It's important. About—" he looked up and down the hall "—the mole.''

"Right. We want to talk to you, too. Just give us a minute, okay?''

"Well, don't be any longer, huh? Because this really is important.''

"We'll be there as soon as we can.'' Cade waited while Harlan walked the few steps to their door, feeling as if he'd been thrown into the middle of some cloak-and-dagger theatrical piece. Then he turned and went back into Talia's room.

"It was Harlan," he told her. "My roommate," he explained to Gerr.

Gerr nodded. "While you were talking to him Talia and I started thinking that calling the cops might not be the best idea just yet. I mean, we've got this jacket, but when they ask Roger if it's his he'll probably say it's not. And that'll be the end of the story.''

Cade nodded. "Maybe you're right. But look, our deliberations start at nine-thirty, so we've got to be down in the conference room by then. And there's something we have to do before that, so...''

"No problem," Gerr said. "But I'm going to have a shot at talking to Roger. I'll see if I can get something more solid on him, and *then* we can call the cops.''

"I don't think that's a good idea," Cade said firmly. "You don't have any idea how he'd react.''

Gerr shrugged. "Even somebody who's mentally unbalanced isn't going to do anything if other people are around. And when I left the dining room Roger had just come in. So I'll go back down and catch him while he's eating. And I'll play it really cool. I'll just start a conversation, with his jacket over my arm, and take it from there. With any luck, he'll get upset enough that—"

"Gerr," Cade interrupted, "the man was shooting at you and Talia last night. Trying to get him upset really doesn't strike me as a rational thing to do."

"Cade's right," Talia said. "It just wouldn't—"

"Hey, will you two relax?" Gerr started for the door. "I'm not going to do anything dumb. And maybe I'll get something to help put this guy away. At any rate, I'll check in with you later."

Cade swore quietly as Gerr headed out. "This is getting really nuts," he muttered. "First Harlan starts playing amateur detective. Now our resident writer's doing it. And somehow they've both hooked themselves up with us—two guys who'd be the last ones I'd pick if we were choosing teams."

"Who would you pick first?" Talia asked. "Roger Podonyi?"

"Very funny." He forced himself to smile, knowing she was only trying to lighten the mood. "You shouldn't have to ask who I'd pick first." He took her in his arms. "And that's why I can't stop worrying about something happening to you before we get out of here," he added, pulling her close and holding her, wishing he never had to let her go.

"Everything's going to be fine," she murmured at last. "All we have to do is go and talk to Bud, put the mistrial wheels in motion."

"Right." Reluctantly he released her. "But first we've got to collect Harlan."

Talia nodded. "I wonder how he's going to feel when we tell him about Roger. I mean, about our finding out who the mole is when he couldn't."

"He's probably not going to be very happy about it. Actually, though, he said he had something important to tell us about the mole."

"Oh? Do you think he found out something? Between the time you snooped on his computer and now?"

"Who knows? But whatever he wants to talk about, we can't let him ramble on. The sooner we see Bud the better. So no messing around, okay?"

Talia gave him a smile so sexy it sent a rush of desire through him. "Can we mess around for just another minute?" She moved closer again.

He reached for her once more, resisting the urge to kiss her. If he did that they might never get around to seeing Bud. So, instead, he simply held her, breathing in the fresh-from-the-shower scent of her hair and thinking how great it was going to be when they were back in the real world.

Once they were they'd have the luxury of enough time to be together. They wouldn't have to settle for only stolen moments. Still, he told himself, closing his eyes, stolen moments were better than none at all.

Chapter Fifteen

The knock on his door made the mole jump. "Yes?" he called, glancing nervously around, checking that both his laptop and cell phone were locked away in his suitcase—even though he knew they were.

"It's Harlan Gates," his visitor announced. "I need to talk to you for a minute."

Wondering what the hell Harlan wanted, the mole opened his door a foot or so.

Harlan pushed his glasses up on his nose and looked into the room. "You're alone, huh? Okay if I come in?"

"Well, actually, I was just getting ready to go down to the conference room."

"This is real important. And there's plenty of time till nine-thirty. I want to show you something," he added, waving the sheets of paper he was holding.

The mole shrugged and opened the door wider. "What's up?" he asked as Harlan came in and pushed the door closed. "What've you got there?"

Harlan didn't say another word. He simply handed over the pages.

It took a single glance at the top one to start the mole sweating. "What's this?" he asked as casually as he could.

"Oh, come on, you know what it is. So let's not fool around."

"How would I know what it is? It's not in English."

"No, it's in code. But I've got another copy that I decoded. And I know you sent the original."

"Sent it where?"

Harlan shrugged. "Okay, have it your way. I just thought you might want to explain it to Bud yourself. It might've made them go easier on you."

"Harlan, I…" He hesitated, trying to quell the sick feeling in his stomach.

He'd known he'd get caught—somehow, by someone. From the day Joey Carpaccio's friends had first come to see him he'd known this was how things would turn out. And he'd also known he'd be dead meat if they did.

He could still hear what Joey's goon had said in that damn washroom: "We don't want no retrial, see?" he'd muttered. "We want this over and done with…. So we're countin' on you to deliver."

But he hadn't delivered. Harlan's discovery meant there *would* be a retrial. And it meant he *was* going to be dead meat—unless he could work something out here.

Maybe Harlan would take a bribe to keep his mouth shut or—

"Don't get any funny ideas," Harlan said. "Because I'm not the only one who knows about this. Cade and Talia do, too. They'd have come with me now, but they got tied up with somebody. And you'd never get away with bumping off all three of us."

The mole wearily shook his head. "Harlan, I could never bump off anybody. I'm not a violent man. I didn't even want to do what I did, but I didn't have any choice, and now... Just give me a minute to think, okay?"

"Think fast."

He tried to do exactly that. If all three of them were on to him he could scrap the idea of bribery. He was sure neither Cade nor Talia were the bribe-taking type. Which really left him with only one option.

All he could do was get the hell out of here. Off this island and right out of South Carolina. Then, if he changed his name, if he started over someplace where nobody could find him, where *Joey* couldn't find him...

He'd thought of that possibility long ago of course. Almost as soon as they'd roped him into doing this. It had to be possible to disappear. The world was a big place, and the Witness Protection Program helped people vanish all the time. So if you had enough brains and money why couldn't you do it on your own?

Oh, he knew it was a long shot. And a last resort. But it looked as if that was all there was left to try.

"Time's up," Harlan announced.

He nodded. "Okay, let's talk about this. Because if I'm going down I don't see any point in going alone."

"WHERE IS HE?" Talia asked when they opened the door and there was no sign of Harlan.

"I don't know." Cade crossed to the bathroom and looked inside, then checked the balcony. "Where the hell would he go?" he muttered.

Talia glanced around the room. Harlan's laptop and printer were in their usual place on the dresser, and beside them were a few sheets of paper, neatly stacked.

She gazed at them for a moment, thinking they hadn't been there last night. "You're sure," she asked, "that he knew he was supposed to wait here for us?"

"Positive. But he obviously got tired of waiting and went somewhere. Maybe he decided to go and talk to Bud without us."

"I can't see him doing that," she said, beginning to feel a little anxious. "Last night, he didn't want *any* of us talking to Bud."

"Well, maybe you're right, but let's find out."

Earlier, they'd checked on what room Bud was in. But when Cade tried the number there was no answer.

"Now what?" Talia said. Her sense that something might be wrong had started growing. "We should try to find Harlan, shouldn't we?"

Cade ran his fingers through his hair, then absently patted his sweater—where it was pulled down over his gun. Seeing that made her more anxious yet.

"I think the best thing to do," he finally said, "is find Bud and talk to him. Get the mistrial wheels in motion as you put it. Then we can worry about Harlan. So I'll go look for Bud and bring him back here and—"

"No, I'll go with you."

"You'll be safer here."

"Cade, I'll be safe with you." And she wanted to be with him. She didn't want anything happening to him, and if Roger had figured out that Cade had voted guilty, too... Well, four eyes watching out for danger were better than two.

"Let's go," she said, starting for the door before he could prolong the argument.

They tried the dining room first, but there was no sign of Bud—and no sign of Roger and Gerr, either.

Their next stop was the conference room. But not only was it empty, a note from their foreman was taped to the door. It said that the deliberations wouldn't be starting until one o'clock and that everyone should make sure they were here by then so they could get going on time.

"On time," Talia said, "was supposed to have been nine-thirty. So why would Myron change that and waste an entire morning?"

"I don't know. It doesn't matter, though, because there aren't going to be any more deliberations. But look, I think we should go back upstairs. We can track Bud down from there."

They headed straight back to Cade's room. Talia had been hoping Harlan might have come back from wherever he'd gone, but he hadn't. And when they tried Bud's room again there was still no answer.

Cade called the desk, asked them to leave a message on Bud's line, then hung up and looked over at Talia. "We're batting a thousand, aren't we. No Bud and no Harlan."

"Well, I'm sure wherever Bud is he's fine, but I can't help worrying that something's happened to Harlan."

"He's probably okay," Cade said, wandering over to Harlan's computer. He picked up the papers sitting beside it and glanced through the first couple.

"Oh, my God," he whispered a few seconds later.

"What?"

"Talia, Harlan found his clue. And Roger might be on Carpaccio's payroll, but he's not the only one. And he's not the mole, either. At least, it wasn't him who sent the E-mail to Joey's people."

"Cade, what on earth are you—"

"Look at this," he interrupted as she hurried over to him. "This is the original encoded E-mail. Harlan's working copy of it, I mean. This writing all over it is his translation. And look how it's mostly in pencil but there's a bit of ink, as if he took two separate shots at it."

"You mean, like one last night and one this morning?"

"Exactly. Maybe by the time he finished last night he was too tired to see anything significant. But then, when he looked at it with fresh eyes this morning...well, just look at what he's got underlined in ink. Look whose name he's written all over the margins."

"Cade, I can't look at anything if you don't hold the paper still."

When he did Talia stared at it in disbelief. The words Harlan had underlined read, "Take a friendly piece of advice about this." And the name written in the margins, neatly circled each time, was Myron.

"Myron?" she murmured. "And you think Harlan's right?"

"I think he's got to be. Myron's always telling people to take a friendly piece of advice."

"Yes, it does add up, doesn't it. I mean, Myron fell all over himself volunteering to be jury foreman, and this explains why. It put him in a perfect position to influence the rest of us."

"Roger *and* Myron," Cade muttered. "Both of them working for Carpaccio. One who knows computers and one who's a crack shot. And they had things so organized they even ended up as roommates."

Talia nodded, staring at the page again. Suddenly Cade muttered a curse.

"What?" she said, looking up.

"What if that's where Harlan went?" Cade said. "What if he went to confront Myron in his room?"

"Oh, Lord," she whispered. "He might have. And I can't imagine Myron being violent, but if Roger was there too..."

"I'll go check it out," Cade said, starting off as he spoke.

"Not without me." Heart pounding, she hurried after him.

"GET AWAY from the door," Cade ordered, pulling Talia against the wall beside him. He wished she'd stayed safely in the room, but there'd been no time to argue with her. Cautiously he reached past the door frame and knocked. There wasn't a sound from inside. He knocked a second time, then called, "Myron? Myron, it's Cade Hailey. I've got to talk to you."

Still no response.

"Myron," he tried again, "I know you're in there, so open up. This is important."

"Just a second."

"That's Harlan!" Talia whispered.

"Don't move. When that door opens, don't move an inch." Cade waited, his adrenaline pumping like crazy. For all he knew, Roger was in there holding a gun on Harlan.

But when the door opened and Harlan peered out he didn't look as if his life was in imminent danger. He was clearly upset, though.

"You okay?" Cade said quietly.

Harlan nodded.

"Who else is in there?"

"Nobody. Only me."

Cade grabbed Talia's hand and hustled her inside. "Okay, what's the deal?" he said once he'd shoved the door closed and snapped it locked.

"Myron's the mole," Harlan told them.

"We know. We looked at what you decoded. But where is he?"

"Well . . . I'm not exactly sure."

"What do you mean, you're not—"

"Cade?" Talia interrupted, squeezing his hand. "Take it easy. Harlan, what's going on?"

Harlan swallowed so hard his Adam's apple bobbed. "Well," he finally said, "Myron went down to the conference room to put a note on the door saying—"

"We know that, too," Cade snapped. "But where did he go from there?"

"I don't know. He said he'd be right back, but that was a while ago." Harlan glanced at his watch. "In fact, it was over half an hour ago, so I don't know what's keeping him."

"Let me get this straight." Cade paused, telling himself to calm down before his blood pressure went through the ceiling. "Did you come here and tell Myron you knew he was the mole?"

Harlan nodded. "I waited for you two to get done with that writer guy. But the time kept dragging on, and it got so late I figured Myron would be going down to the conference room soon."

"Okay. So you told him you knew and he said...?"

"Well, at first he pretended not to know what I was talking about. But then he admitted he was."

"And were there just the two of you in the room? Or was Roger here?"

"No, only Myron and me."

Cade glanced at Talia, making sure she'd registered the significance of that. At least Roger didn't know they were on to anything yet—unless old Gerr had spilled the beans, which was a distinct possibility.

"All right," he said, focusing on Harlan again. "After you told Myron you knew he was the mole, then what? How did he end up just walking out of here?"

"Well . . ." Harlan's nervous glances were starting to make him look like a terrified rabbit. "It wasn't that Myron just *walked* out of here," he said at last. "It was that we needed to buy some time, and he came up with the idea of the note. By saying the deliberations wouldn't be starting till later, we had the whole morning."

"What's with this *we* stuff?" Cade demanded. "You joined forces with Myron? To do what?"

"Cade," Talia said quietly, "you're asking him a dozen questions at once." She looked at Harlan. "What did you and Myron need time for?"

"To find out who's been trying to kill you."

"What?" Cade practically yelled.

"Cade . . ." Talia said warningly.

When he looked at her this time he wished he hadn't. She was apparently getting awfully annoyed, because the tight smile she gave him was more like a death threat than anything even remotely friendly.

"Why don't we try just letting Harlan tell this his own way," she said tersely. "Go ahead, Harlan."

"Well, see, Myron was really upset about that guy shooting at you."

"But Myron's been part of things all along, so why would he be upset?" Cade asked. "And he *knows* who's been trying to kill her. It's Roger."

"Roger? Roger Podony? No, that can't be right, because Myron said it had to be a hired killer. A pro."

"Harlan," Talia said, "we're positive it's Roger, but let's not worry about that right now. Fill us in on the rest of what happened with Myron, okay?"

"There isn't much more. Once he knew I was on to him he said that if he was going down he didn't see the point in going alone. He said we should find out who the hired killer was."

"But why?" Talia asked. "If Myron's working for Joey Carpaccio why did he suggest double-crossing him?"

"Because he said he didn't know they'd be trying to kill you. And if he had he'd never have gotten involved. I mean, he never wanted to get involved even *without* knowing about that. But they made him."

"How?"

"Joey Carpaccio has something on him."

When Harlan simply stood there, not volunteering any more information, Cade could have cheerfully killed him. Talia, though, patiently asked him to elaborate.

"Well, you know how Myron's got that big job?" Harlan began. "Vice president of his company?"

She nodded.

"Well, he used to be a vice president of a bank. Out in California. But he got fired a few years back. Somebody embezzled a ton of money from the bank and they blamed him. He said it was all a misunderstanding, but I got the feeling that might not be true."

"Was he charged?" Cade asked.

"No. And he said that was because he was innocent, which meant they didn't have any evidence. But you know how banks are. Maybe they just didn't prosecute so nobody would hear what had happened, just didn't want to hurt their reputation."

"And after that he came to Charleston?" Talia asked.

"Uh-huh. Nobody in Charleston knew the story. But when he ended up on the jury…well, Joey's guys obviously wanted somebody they could blackmail. So I guess they started looking for dirt on all the jurors and found out about Myron's bank thing."

"So Joey's guys," Talia concluded, "told Myron that either he went along with them or they'd make sure his new employers heard about it."

Harlan nodded. "But now that he's going to get charged with…with whatever jury moles get charged with, he'll lose his job anyway."

"Not to mention that he'll end up in jail," Cade muttered.

"Right. So that's why he figured he might as well at least find out who's been trying to kill Talia. Get *him* sent to jail, too."

Cade resisted the impulse to point out, again, that it was Roger. And to point out that Myron had obviously strung Harlan a line.

But Harlan must have caught something in his expression, because he said, "See, Talia, even though I know Cade doesn't believe me Myron really didn't know anybody was going to be trying to kill you. And he feels awfully bad about it."

"So how was he going to figure out who this killer is?" Cade asked, curious to hear exactly what Myron's explanation had been.

"Well," Harlan said, "he got out his cell phone right then and there, and he phoned this contact he's got."

"The contact is one of Joey's boys?" Talia asked.

Harlan nodded. "See, Joey wants a verdict of not guilty. He doesn't want a hung jury. So Myron was going to say the jurors had decided they'd never be able to agree. That we were agitating to take a final vote so we could call it quits and go home."

"And?"

"And then Myron was going to say that he needed to know who the killer was, that he had to talk to him so he'd know to get his job done fast, before we took the vote."

Cade just stood looking at Harlan, wondering how he could possibly have bought a story with so many holes in it.

"I think I'm missing some of the logic in this," Talia said. "What good would it've done to get rid of me before the vote?"

"Well, Myron was going to say that with you dead he'd be able to get everyone else to vote not guilty. That he'd be able to convince the rest of us that either we did it or we'd all end up dead, too."

"Harlan?" Cade said, deciding he'd heard enough. "You keep saying, 'Myron was going to,' which means he didn't. So what happened?"

"Well, when he phoned his contact the guy wasn't there. So all he could do was leave a message telling him to get back to him right away. Then he went downstairs to put his note on the door. But...well, as we've all noticed, he hasn't come back."

"And where's his cell phone? Did he take it with him?"

"Uh-uh. He was going to, but I made him leave it here. That way I'd know if his guy called. It's right over there." Harlan pointed to where it was lying on a chair. "Making him leave it was the smart thing to do, wasn't it?"

"Yeah, that was the smart thing to do." And if only Harlan had started using his brain before that point, Myron wouldn't be long gone. Cade headed over and picked up the phone, then pushed the "send" button.

"What are you doing?" Talia asked.

"When you push 'send' without dialing a number, "it acts like a 'redial' button. So let's just see what we get at the number of Myron's *contact.*"

Once the connection was made he listened for a few seconds, then growled, "Terrific. His contact is a computer that gives out the time and temperature."

He disconnected, then punched the operator button and waited impatiently until someone answered. "I need the Charleston Harbor Police," he told her. "This is an emergency.

"Myron," he added, glancing at Talia, "didn't give a damn about whether you got killed or not. He just figured he could buy himself a few hours' head start.

I'll bet that after he taped that note to the door he headed straight for the village marina.''

"You think he's running?"

Cade nodded. "I'd say he's on a boat right now, halfway to Charleston.''

Chapter Sixteen

After Cade had finished with the Harbor Police and was trying Bud's room, Talia turned to Harlan and said softly, "Don't blame yourself for what happened with Myron."

When he stopped pacing and glanced over at her she could see he was still incredibly upset.

"Don't blame myself?" he echoed. "Who else is there to blame? If I hadn't been so stupid Myron wouldn't be on his way to Charleston."

"But if you hadn't been so smart nobody would ever have known we had a mole on the jury, let alone figured out who it was. So maybe you did make a mistake, but you blew everything wide open before that happened. And everyone's entitled to an occasional mistake."

"Well . . . I guess. That's what my mom tells me all the time."

"You see? Mothers are always right. Besides, I'm sure the Harbor Police will catch up with Myron. Then you'll be a hero."

"Yeah? You really think that's how it'll turn out?"

She nodded, but Harlan looked only half-convinced and went back to his pacing. After watching him for a few seconds she let her thoughts wander to Roger. Myron might be on a boat halfway to Charleston, but Roger was still right here at Bride's Bay. And Myron's insisting it was a hired killer who'd shot at her last night didn't make it true. The evidence added up to Roger.

Taking a deep breath, she told herself to stop thinking about hired killers and evidence. It was safe to stop playing Nancy Drew now. She, Cade and Harlan had found out everything they needed to know. All that was left to do was get hold of Bud and tell him the story.

After that, the excitement would officially be over and she'd be able to relax. Which was just as well. She didn't think she could take much more of life on the edge.

Then Cade hung up and shook his head. "Still no answer in Bud's room."

His words started her stomach churning. Where on earth *was* the man? She began imagining him lying dead in a spreading pool of blood just like Mrs. Wertman, and a little shiver ran through her. Silently muttering a few nasty words to her imagination, she forced her attention to Cade once more.

"So," he was saying, "let's get out of here before Roger shows up. We can try Bud again from our own rooms and..." His words trailed off at the sound of a key in the lock.

When the door opened Talia's throat filled with fear. Roger Podonyi was standing there staring at them angrily. From the corner of her eye, she saw Cade's hand move to his waist. Then she looked at Roger again, wondering if he'd seen the motion, too. Wondering if he could tell Cade had a gun concealed. Wondering if *he* had a gun somewhere....

Suddenly she knew how it would feel to be in the showdown scene from *High Noon*. Only this scene was playing out in real life. Her heart racing, she prayed it wouldn't turn into real death.

"What's going on?" Roger finally demanded when none of them said a word. "Where's Myron? And what are you three doing in here?"

Talia's breathing stopped and her mind went blank. She couldn't have come up with an answer if her life had depended on it. And maybe her life *did* depend on it.

Then Cade began casually walking toward her, his eyes on Roger. "We're just waiting for Myron."

He sounded so calm she almost started breathing again.

"Have you seen him?" he added as he reached her side.

"No." Roger closed the door and started forward. "I figured he'd be here. But why were the deliberations delayed? Did he tell you?"

Harlan cleared his throat; Talia quickly shot him a warning glance. The less any of them said the better—especially him.

"He told Harlan he was coming back after he put up his note," Cade said. "But he's obviously been delayed, so I guess we'd better get going. We can catch him later, and we don't want to be in your way here."

Roger shrugged. "Stay if you want. I'm going right back out. I just need something." He slid open the closet door, reached in and pulled out his denim jacket.

Talia's gaze flashed to Cade. The last time they'd seen that jacket, Gerr had been walking out of her room with it over his arm. The look Cade gave her said he didn't know what the story could be, either.

"So," he said as Roger headed across the room, "you got your jacket back from Gerr, huh?"

"What?" Roger paused, glancing over at him.

"Ah...nothing."

Roger turned away and opened the top drawer of the dresser. When he shoved it closed again and turned around he was holding a gun.

Talia stood frozen, her gaze glued to the gun, her brain pounding with the horrifying certainty that they were about to die. Roger had probably killed Gerr because he'd found that jacket. And now he was going to kill them.

Then, faintly, she heard an imaginary voice asking why Roger was pointing his gun at the floor, not at one of them. Just as she began wondering about that, she caught a motion out of the corner of her eye. By the time she turned to look, Cade had his Browning trained on Roger. He stared at it, his face draining of color.

"Put it down," Cade ordered, gesturing at Roger's gun with his own. "Very slowly."

Without a word Roger carefully bent over and set his gun on the floor.

"Now kick it under the chair."

As he did that Cade lowered the Browning to his side. Roger straightened, saw it was no longer aimed at him and began looking only half as frightened.

"Okay, what's going on?" he said. "Is this supposed to be funny or what?"

"None of us want to end up dead," Cade told him. "That's what's going on."

"Dead," he repeated. "Don't tell me you thought I was going to shoot you."

"When somebody pulls a gun it's been known to happen."

Talia was certain Roger had a sarcastic retort on the tip of his tongue. Then he clearly thought better of antagonizing a man with a semiautomatic in his hand.

"Hell, Cade," he said with a nervous smile, "I only got out the gun because I'm on my way to the shooting range."

"Sure," Cade said.

"Have a look at it. It's not loaded. I never leave it loaded."

"Do you want me to get it?" Talia asked.

When Cade nodded she gingerly retrieved it from under the chair and handed it over. "Empty," he muttered after a moment.

"See?" Roger said. "I've only got a few rounds, and they're in my suitcase. I was going to buy a box or two of bullets at the range."

Cade's eyes flickered to Talia. He held her gaze for a moment, silently asking what she thought.

She gave him an uncertain shrug. If Roger hadn't, in fact, murdered Gerr, then Gerr must have willingly given that jacket back to him. Which would mean Roger'd had an explanation for its being by the road this morning. And maybe he *had* only gotten out his gun because he was on his way to the shooting range.

But if he had an explanation about that jacket... She mentally shook her head. *Had* he been the one shooting at her last night or not?

"Why don't you call down to the concierge and check out my story?" he suggested. "As soon as I read Myron's note I asked Joanie to reserve me an hour on the range."

Cade turned to Harlan. "Phone down and check."

Harlan's hand was trembling so badly that the receiver slipped when he first picked it up, but he eventually got hold of Joanie and asked if she'd made the reservation.

"She did," he said, hanging up. "She thought I was Roger, and she said they were expecting me right now."

"So?" Roger said. "You all satisfied?"

"Yeah," Cade replied. "And look, I'm sorry about this. But after last night... well, I'm sorry."

Roger shrugged, his forced-looking smile encompassing the three of them. "Hey, these things happen. You see a gun and you sometimes jump to the wrong conclusions. So, if you'll just give it to me I'll catch you all in the conference room at one.''

When Cade handed it over Roger silently started for the door. Talia watched him leave, certain he wouldn't have been nearly as understanding if Cade wasn't still holding a loaded gun.

''Why did you let him go?'' Harlan demanded the instant Roger was gone. ''If you two are so sure he was the one doing the shooting last night why didn't we call the police while he was right here? We could've held him for them.''

Cade sighed. ''I'm a construction engineer, not a special agent. And as far as being sure he's the one goes...''

''*Are* you still sure?'' Talia asked. ''When I saw that jacket I wished we'd touched base with Gerr again.''

Cade nodded. ''The only thing I'm sure about right now is that we've got to get you off this island in one piece.''

''If you want anyone to second that thought,'' she murmured, ''I'm right here.''

''I know.'' His gaze held hers long enough to tell her that *right here* was exactly where he wanted her. It gave her such a warm feeling she actually managed a smile.

''If Roger *is* guilty of anything,'' he said, glancing at Harlan, ''he won't get away with it. Once we've talked to Bud he'll contact all the authorities who should be involved—including the sheriff's depart-

ment. So let's head back to our own rooms and have
another shot at phoning him.''

WHEN THEY TURNED into their hallway Gerald Asimov was standing outside Talia's door. Cade told
himself not to let it annoy him, but he really wished
the guy would get lost.

''That's your writer friend, isn't it?'' Harlan asked.

Talia nodded, then glanced at Cade. ''He probably
wants to tell us what happened when he talked to
Roger. So at least that mystery will be solved.''

''He talked to Roger?'' Harlan repeated. ''How
come?''

''It's kind of a long story,'' Talia said just as Gerr
glanced along the hall and spotted them. ''We'll fill
you in later—okay?—because Gerr doesn't know all
the facts.''

''Yeah,'' Cade said, ''and let's make this quick. At
the rate we're going,'' he added, as they neared Gerr,
''Bud'll have retired before we track him down.''

''You've been looking for Bud?'' Gerr said.

Cade mentally kicked himself. He hadn't realized
his words would carry that far, and the fewer topics up
for discussion the faster Gerr would be gone.

''Well, that answers my question,'' he said. ''I was
wondering where you were. I tried to catch you before your deliberations started, so I saw that note. And
I've been looking all over for you since then.''

''Actually we've been talking to Harlan here,'' Cade
said, introducing them. ''So,'' he continued, focusing
on Gerr again, ''what happened with Roger?''

"With Roger?"

"We ran into him," Talia said. "And he had his jacket back."

"Oh. His jacket." Gerr shrugged, his glance flickering meaningfully in Harlan's direction.

"It's okay," Talia told him. "Harlan knows about Roger."

"Oh. Well, then, what happened was Roger looked me straight in the eye and thanked me for finding it."

"He didn't try to explain what it was doing by the road?" Cade said.

"Uh-uh. He acted surprised when I told him where it was—gave me a story about how somebody stole it while he was checking in the other day. Said he left it lying on his briefcase and it disappeared."

"Then it just *happened* to turn up behind a bush?" Cade said. "Right near where he *happened* to be last night? How dumb did he think you were?"

"I don't know, but I wasn't dumb enough to push it with him. Hell, I just write about murder victims. I've got no interest in becoming one. At any rate, I was wondering if maybe you and Talia wouldn't mind talking to me about my book for an hour or so. You too, Harlan, if you'd like. I don't know if anybody mentioned what I'm working on, but—"

"Look," Cade interrupted, "normally we'd be glad to help you out, but we can't right now."

"We really do have to get hold of Bud," Harlan put in. "Jury stuff."

"Yeah." Gerr nodded knowingly. "I figured you'd decide you had to tell him about Roger. I mean, trying to kill one of his fellow jurors? He's given a whole new meaning to the term jury misconduct.''

Cade nodded. "Exactly. So we really can't sit and talk just now.''

"Yeah, I understand. Well, good luck finding Bud.''

"Seems like a nice guy," Harlan said as Gerr headed down the hall.

"Not nearly as nice as some I know," Talia whispered, giving Cade a smile.

ONCE THE THREE OF THEM were in Talia's room Cade began phoning Bud again. It took a few tries, but eventually he got an answer.

He resisted the impulse to shout hallelujah and settled for giving Talia and Cade a thumbs-up. "Bud, it's Cade Hailey. I've been trying to get you.''

"Yeah, I got the message you left, but the whole world's been trying to get me. Every time I take two steps somebody stops me to ask what happened to the deliberations this morning. And I should know the answer, but that darned Myron Beyers didn't have the decency to tell me anything.''

"Well, that's part of what I've got to talk to you about.''

"Oh. Okay, but things have been really hectic, and I'm just walking out the door again. So I'll get back to you in a while, all right?''

"No, that's not all right. This is urgent.''

"Well, I'm supposed to be meeting the Judge, and I'm already late so—''

"*Urgent,* Bud. As in, it can't wait."

"Oh. Then I guess . . . No, hold on, I've got a better idea. You work in construction, right? Isn't that what you told me?"

"More or less. Mostly renovations but—"

"Doesn't matter. You'll still be a lot more help than me. See, the Judge has a problem. And I offered to have a look at it 'cause I was in construction way back. Maybe I told you about it."

"No, I don't think you did," Cade said, wishing Bud would come to the point.

"I know a lot has changed since then," Bud went on. "So much new building material and stuff. So why don't you meet me, and we can talk and have a look at this thing with the Judge at the same time."

Cade hesitated. But at this point it could hardly matter if they talked in front of somebody. Especially not the Judge. "Fine," he said. "Where do I meet you?"

"Well, if you go past the dining room you'll see a door on your left. It opens onto stairs, and you want to take them down to the basement. Then go along the hall past the kitchen and the staff cafeteria. At the end it turns, and you'll come to a door that says 'No admittance'."

"Okay, I'll—"

"You're going to be interested in what's beyond that door," Bud went on. "It's an old tunnel that leads almost to the bay."

"Yeah? The bartender was mentioning something about a couple of tunnels the other day. So I'll see you down there in—"

"This one dates back to the time of pirates and smugglers," Bud interrupted, always the storyteller. "The island plantations used to get some of their supplies from those guys."

"And the Judge's problem has something to do with the tunnel?" Cade said, trying to get Bud back on track.

"Uh-huh. There's kind of a storage area about halfway along that's a lot wider than the rest of it. And the Judge is worried it's giving away there. Figures they could suddenly have a sinkhole on the property. So we'll just have a look at it for him. Hell, maybe your company could even do the work fixing it. How about we say in ten minutes?"

"Fine." He hung up before Bud could start in on anything else.

"What's happening?" Talia asked.

He quickly explained. "So," he concluded, "I'll head down there and you two just sit tight. I shouldn't be long."

"I'm going with you," she said.

"There's no reason to."

"There's no reason not to."

For a second he thought about arguing, but she was wearing a stubborn expression that told him there was no point. Besides, he'd just as soon have her with him as be worrying about her the whole time he was gone.

"All right," he said. "And what about you, Harlan? You're the one who discovered we had a leak on the jury. You should be the one to tell Bud the details."

"Well...maybe I'll wait and do it later. I've got kind of a problem with things like tunnels and caves. So I think I'll just go back to our room. Maybe call my mom and let her know I'll be home by tonight."

Cade nodded, then glanced at Talia. They'd all be home by tonight. And given the way she was looking at him, tonight couldn't come soon enough.

Chapter Seventeen

The chef and her staff, Talia noted in passing, were so busy getting ready for lunch that nobody even glanced up as she and Cade walked by the kitchen. Which was probably just as well. There'd been a sign on the stairway door saying Hotel Employees Only.

"You still hanging in okay?" Cade murmured, squeezing her hand.

She smiled in reply. "So far so good. I'm not one of those women who always imagines killers in basements. But do you want to know a secret?"

"Sure."

"Harlan isn't the only one who has a problem with things like tunnels and caves."

"Really? Then why didn't you stay upstairs with him?"

"Well, partly because I know you should face up to things you're afraid of."

"And partly...?"

She smiled at him again. "I'd far rather be with you than with Harlan, regardless of where."

That made him grin. "How much is *far* rather?"

"Oh . . . how does a million times sound?"

"It'll do for starters." He released her hand and drapped his arm over her shoulders. "According to Bud, the tunnel entrance is just beyond the corner up ahead, so we're almost there."

And that meant this entire ordeal was almost over. After they talked to Bud, they'd be on their way home in no time.

She glanced at Cade once more, thanking her lucky stars they'd both come through this safely. Then she thanked fate for sending him to her.

Until he'd appeared in her life, she'd never known how absolutely wonderful being in love could be. But now she did. And even though it seemed impossible, given everything that had happened, she only had to look at him to feel happy all over again. Her million times hadn't been an exaggeration. Being with him made her feel as if she was floating on air, and she wanted to be with him for the rest of her life.

When they turned the corner Bud was waiting at a door posted No Admittance. "Well, there you are, Cade," he said. "And I see you brought Talia along."

"I won't get in the way," she promised.

He smiled, but he looked so anxious she decided he couldn't like tunnels any more than she or Harlan. "If it's okay with you," he said, glancing at Cade, "we'll talk after we've finished with the Judge. He's gone on ahead, because the lighting in the tunnel's real old and you've got to switch it on in a couple of different places.

"We'll have to walk single file," he added, opening the door and gesturing for Cade to go first. "It's pretty narrow in there."

Talia followed Cade into the tunnel. The floor was hard-packed sand, and the ceiling and walls were shored with ancient timbers and lined with bricks that wore a century's accumulation of grime and cobwebs.

Then the door closed behind them and she couldn't see how dingy everything was. In fact, she couldn't see much at all. Bud hadn't exaggerated about the lighting being old. The tunnel wasn't pitch-black, but the light was nothing more than a gloomy twilight.

"I hope the Judge has a good flashlight with him," Cade muttered, "or trying to look at his problem is going to be an exercise in futility."

"He's got one of those big lantern types," Bud told them.

Talia stuck close behind Cade as they walked on, trying not to think about the possibility of the tunnel's caving in. Or about bats. Or snakes. The snakes proved the hardest to get out of her mind, because somebody had spotted a couple of water moccasins when their ferry had docked the other day. She tried taking a deep, calming breath, but the tunnel was so musty she sneezed.

Telling herself this was wonderful desensitization therapy, she kept walking. But with each step the air felt more clammy against her skin. All in all, she was starting to wish she *had* stayed upstairs with Harlan.

"How much farther?" Cade asked, glancing back.

"I think we're almost there," Bud assured him. "The Judge said the wider bit is just beyond the first bend, and I can see that up ahead."

Talia peered past Cade through the semidarkness, wondering how a man almost at retirement age could see better than she could. Then she managed to make out the bend, too, courtesy of the beam of light up ahead. That had to be where the Judge was waiting with his flashlight. The tunnel began to widen as they neared the bend, and the beam grew brighter. Then they turned the corner and Cade stopped so suddenly she almost banged into him.

Reaching out, she rested her hand on the reassuring solidness of his back. She was in need of a little reassurance, because she couldn't see a thing now. Nothing except his dark shape in front of her and white light all around him.

"Jeez," he muttered, "that light's blinding, Judge. Could you aim the flashlight down?"

"In a minute. But what do we have here? You didn't come alone, Cade."

Talia's heart started to pound. That voice didn't belong to the Judge.

CADE SQUINTED into the glare from the flashlight, his adrenaline pumping wildly and his brain desperately trying to put an identity to the voice. A name was lurking in the front of his mind, but it refused to click into place.

"I didn't have any idea Talia would come with him," Bud was babbling. "He didn't tell me she was. She just showed up."

"It's okay—a stroke of luck, in fact. She's the one I really want. Just figured I had to get rid of him first 'cause he was sticking so close to her. But doing both of them at once'll be fine."

The words made Cade's stomach lurch and his blood run cold. He couldn't see a damn thing, but *doing both of them* had to mean the flashlight wasn't the only thing pointed at them.

Who was this guy? The name that went with the voice finally came to him. The man behind the light was Gerald Asimov. *He* was Carpaccio's hired gun!

Before that realization even had a chance to sink in, a thousand more questions surfaced. What kind of pistol did Gerr have? What kind of bullets? Ones that would explode in Cade's body and kill only him? Or ones that would tear right through and hit Talia before she could even try to make a run for it?

Not that she'd have much of a chance, but if he could somehow give her even a few seconds...

He tried to think, intensely aware of the Browning still snugged against his waist. But how was he going to get at it when Gerr had him in a damn spotlight?

When he started to raise his hand to shield his eyes Gerr snapped, "Don't move."

"All right," he said as evenly as he could. "But what do you want?"

"Take off, Bud," Gerr ordered, ignoring the question. "And make sure you lock the door behind you. I'll be going out the other end."

"Bud?" Talia whispered, her voice so terror-filled it tore at Cade's heart. "Bud, why did you do this? Why on earth would you help him?"

"Everyone's got their price," Gerr said before Bud could utter a word. "Including your court officer here. His was enjoying his retirement years a lot more than he'd hoped, right Bud?"

"Right," he mumbled.

"And you've earned every penny I paid you. Did you two like the way he avoided you all morning to give me time? And I'll bet you never dreamed it was him shooting at us last night, did you, Talia."

"But... you mean it wasn't Roger?"

"That's right. He was only out for a walk, just like he said. I set up the shooting with Bud. Figured I'd get as big a kick out of scaring you that way as I did in the hall the other night."

"What about Roger's jacket?" Cade demanded—anything to buy time.

"You mean *my* jacket," Gerr said. "Roger had *his* jacket all along. See, I didn't really go to Talia's room to show her any jacket this morning."

"You went there to kill her," Cade muttered, wondering how he could have been so damn stupid.

"Right," Gerr admitted. "But when you were there, I had to come up with a cover. And saying I'd found Roger's jacket was it. That's enough of this talk, though. Bud, I already told you to get out of here."

Without another word Bud started away, the soft thud of his footsteps rapidly fading into nothingness.

"So here we are," Gerr said quietly. "Just the three of us. Step out from behind Cade, Talia. Out where I can see you."

As she slowly moved to his side Cade tried to come up with a plan. He had to do something. He couldn't just let the woman he loved die. But his brain refused to cooperate, and all he could think to do was wrap his arm around her trembling shoulders.

"Now isn't that touching," Gerr sneered.

"Why are you doing this?" Talia asked. "You're obviously an intelligent man. Why kill people for a living? Why work for Joey Carpaccio?"

Gerr chuckled. "I don't kill people for a living, Talia. I really *am* a lawyer, although the writer part wasn't true. And I don't have a thing to do with Joey Carpaccio. As far as I know he's never had anyone trying to kill you. I'm doing this strictly for myself, just for the pure pleasure of revenge."

"Revenge? But I don't even know you."

"Oh, but you do. At least, you know *of* me. Not as Gerald Asimov, but how about as Trent McNally?"

When she didn't answer Gerr finally lowered the flashlight a little. Cade blinked, trying to eliminate the glare that still danced in front of his eyes. Gradually his vision cleared enough to let him see the semiautomatic in Gerr's other hand. It was a little .38, but plenty big enough. And he had it aimed straight at Talia.

"The name Trent McNally doesn't ring any bells, Talia?" Gerr said at last. "You don't remember Linda McNally talking about her husband?"

"You're Linda's husband?" she whispered.

"What's the story?" Cade said, casually taking his arm from around her shoulders and edging away an inch. If he could get some distance between them, things might be just a bit tougher for old Gerr.

"I... Cade, I don't know what the story is," Talia replied. "I counseled Linda McNally at the women's shelter, but—"

"You *counseled* her," Gerr interjected. "You call telling her I was an abusive husband counseling her?"

"I hardly had to *tell* her," Talia said quietly.

"Dammit, I never laid a finger on her unless she deserved it. But you got hold of her and the next thing I knew she was out the door."

"Leaving you was her decision, not mine."

"Like hell. You convinced her to take off. And where did that leave me, huh? Did you even give a thought to that?"

Cade kept his eyes glued on Gerr. The guy so obviously wanted to make sure Talia knew why she was going to die that maybe he'd get careless about keeping the gun aimed at her. But the longer he talked the less it looked as if that was going to happen.

"Did it even occur to you," he went on, his face dark with anger, "what being labeled a wife beater does to a family lawyer's reputation? To his practice? Well, I'll tell you, Ms. Counselor. Thanks to you, I had to leave Charleston. I'm living up in Greenville now, having to build a whole new practice."

"Killing Talia isn't going to make your new practice grow any faster," Cade said evenly. "And it's not going to get your wife back, either."

"Maybe not," Gerr snapped, "but it's going to make me feel one helluva lot better."

"Only until you get caught."

"But I won't. I had everything planned perfectly weeks ago. Then all I had to do was wait till the trial ended and book myself into the right hotel. Hell, when they reached the final arguments I made reservations at every place they could possibly send you."

"You'll still get caught," Cade said calmly, trying to sound more confident than he felt.

"Yeah? Well, I really doubt that. Who's the obvious one to blame when Talia turns up dead? Some lawyer from New York who went home before her body was even discovered? People won't even think about me, because they'll automatically blame Carpaccio. Figure he wanted rid of the only woman juror—and that you just happened to be with her at the time."

"Except that Harlan knows we came down here to meet Bud," Talia said, her voice quavery a little. "And Bud can't keep quiet to save his life. So when they question him he'll tell them everything."

"Wishful thinking," Gerr said. A flicker of doubt crossed his face, though, and Cade seized the moment.

He dove forward, slashing at Gerr's gun hand. The gun went off, its blast exploding and reverberating. Before Gerr could regain his balance Cade drove his fist deep into Gerr's stomach. The lawyer doubled over with an anguished cry, and Cade swiped at the gun again, this time knocking it free.

A moment later he had his own gun out. But the excruciating pain in his hand told him he'd broken something. As he tried to aim, Gerr's leg swung in a wide kick that didn't stop until his foot connected with the Browning.

The gun went flying, sending a fresh surge of pain from Cade's hand right up to his shoulder. He did his best to ignore it and stared at Gerr, the sound of their ragged breathing filling the tunnel. "No guns now," he said.

"Maybe not," Gerr said. Then his hand flashed down to his boot and came back up holding a knife. "But that doesn't mean things are even."

Cade's throat went dry. With a broken hand he didn't have a chance.

Then Talia said quietly, "You're right, Gerr. Things *aren't* even."

Cade glanced at her. "Nice work," he said, positive that he was going to love her forever. She'd gotten the Browning and had it trained on Gerr.

"You don't have the guts," Gerr snarled.

"Try me," she said.

TALIA AND CADE, along with the Judge and Liz Jermain, walked the detectives and their prisoners down to the hotel marina. The other jurors had left on the evening ferry, but Boscoe and Rebuzo hadn't been quite finished with Talia and Cade by seven o'clock, so a private boat was waiting to take them back to Charleston.

As the Harbor Police cruiser pulled away into the gathering twilight, Frank Boscoe turned and raised his hand in farewell. Arnie Rebuzo had already gone below to keep an eye on Bud and Gerr—or Bud and Trent McNally, to be accurate. Talia waved goodbye to Boscoe, then looked up at Cade and smiled. He hadn't waved. His left arm was wrapped tightly around her shoulders. And his right hand, pending X rays on the mainland, was temporarily immobilized by splints, courtesy of a doctor who lived in the estates.

"We haven't seen the last of Bud and Gerr, you know," he said above the peaceful lapping of the water. "We're going to be star witnesses at their trials. And at Myron's, too."

She nodded. As they'd hoped, the Harbor Police had intercepted their jury foreman when he'd reached Charleston. Myron had been in custody for hours.

"I thought those detectives were never going to stop asking questions," the Judge complained to Liz. Then he turned to Talia and Cade, shaking his head ruefully.

"I just don't know how we can apologize to you two. Believe me, nobody in the history of the Bride's Bay Resort has ever had an experience like yours."

"We lived through it," Talia told him. "That's the main thing."

"But would you ever feel brave enough to come back?" Liz asked. "After we've hired a new security chief, I mean."

Talia smiled again. She was with Cade and she was safe. And the terror she'd felt mere hours ago had faded. "I think," she said at last, "I might make a point of coming back someday. It would be nice to stay here under different circumstances."

"Well," Liz said, "if you're serious about that we'd be delighted to have you. Both of you—on the house of course. We've got a suite you'd absolutely love."

"She doesn't mean you'd have to come together and share the suite," the Judge put in quickly. "She just means she'd like you to have our best accommodations."

"Yes, that's exactly what I meant," Liz agreed, shooting Talia a smile that said she suspected they wouldn't mind coming together and sharing. "The suite I've got in mind is booked for the president in a couple of months, but anytime before or after, it's yours for the asking."

"Thanks," Cade said. "We'll keep that in mind. But right now, I guess we'd better get going."

They all started along the dock, Liz and the Judge in the lead. When the two of them paused to talk to the skipper of the boat that would be taking Cade and Talia to the mainland, Cade stopped and turned to face her.

"Tell me something," he said quietly.

"What?"

"Back there in the tunnel would you really have shot Gerr?"

"Absolutely. If he'd made a move I'd have shot him in a second. I certainly wouldn't have let him stick a knife in you."

Cade grinned. "You know, I've spent my entire adult life wishing I had a woman who wouldn't let someone stick a knife in me. It's a terrific quality."

"I have a lot of terrific qualities," she teased.

"I know. And I also know," he added, turning serious, "that once those three trials are under way things could be awfully hectic for us."

She nodded.

"So I was thinking...if there's anything important we want to do it would make sense to do it soon, before that happens. Before things get hectic, I mean."

"Anything important like what?" she murmured.

Instead of answering, he leaned forward and kissed her—a long loving kiss that gave her a pretty fair idea of what he had in mind.

"Anything important like getting married," he finally whispered. "And getting away on a honeymoon. Talia, I realize it's fast, and we haven't even met each other's families. But does that matter when I love you like crazy?"

"You can meet my parents tomorrow," she replied, certain nothing mattered except that he loved her and she loved him.

"Good, because I don't want to spend another minute of my life without you. I want to marry you soon, okay?"

She nodded again, happy tears filling her eyes. The worst experience in her entire life had just turned into the best.

"So the wedding," she said, trying to blink back those tears. "Just how soon did you have in mind?"

"The sooner the better."

The way he was gazing at her, as if he wished it could be tonight, made her certain she was the luckiest woman alive.

"And the honeymoon?" she asked. "Did you have any particular place in mind?"

"Judge? Liz?" he called, not taking his eyes from her. "About that presidential suite..."

Epilogue

Bride's Bay Resort offered the perfect setting for an outdoor wedding, and the day had dawned bright and sunny.

Since Cade and Talia's first visit to Jermain Island, the centuries-old live oaks had deepened from the succulent green of spring to the verdant green of summer. The sunlight that filtered softly through the leaves dappled the grass below and breathed warmth into the grayish green of the Spanish moss hanging from the huge branches.

"Nervous?" Cade's brother, Mike, asked him as they stood waiting with the minister.

"No, maybe it's unusual, but I'm completely relaxed." There was no reason not to be, though. He and Talia hadn't even had the stress of planning their wedding. When they'd told Liz Jermain they'd like to spend their honeymoon at Bride's Bay she'd insisted that the wedding be held here, too, and that the hotel staff would take care of everything.

And Liz had outdone herself making the day perfect—from the private boat to bring the wedding guests to the island, to the champagne reception planned for after the ceremony.

But the main reason he wasn't nervous, of course, was that he was so sure about marrying Talia. His love for her had only grown during the weeks since the jury deliberations.

"I still can't get over this," Mike said.

Cade laughed quietly. "Over what? That your brother's getting married in such a classy place?"

"Partly. And partly that you're getting married again at all. For a guy who said he never would, you changed your mind awfully fast when you met Talia."

"You can see why, can't you?"

"Yeah. She's great. The whole family thinks so."

Cade turned to look at his parents. Rows of chairs had been set up on the lawn, and they were sitting in the front row.

As he watched, his mother leaned across his father to say something to Talia's mother. The two women had been busily forming family ties from the moment they'd met.

In the rows behind sat relatives from both sides and close friends, as well as most of the other members of the jury. Somehow it had seemed fitting to invite them.

Myron Beyers wasn't here of course. The judge at his hearing had denied him bail, saying that since he'd already tried to run once he didn't seem like a good risk.

Roger Podonyi hadn't come, either. He'd claimed a previous engagement, but it was more likely he hadn't forgiven Talia and Cade for suspecting him.

All the others were there, though, and the unmarried ones had brought dates. All except Harlan, who'd brought his mother.

Cade eyed him for a minute, glad that he and Talia had made a point of getting together with him in Charleston and apologizing for having ever thought he'd been one of the bad guys. After all, if it hadn't been for Harlan's computer sleuthing, there was no way of knowing how things would have turned out.

The string quartet that was set up under one of the trees stopped playing for a moment. Then it broke into the strains of Mendelssohn's "Wedding March."

"There she is," Mike whispered.

When Cade looked toward the doorway of the old plantation house, his throat grew tight. Talia's best friend, Carol, and Mike's wife, Darlene—the bridesmaid and matron of honor, respectively—had started down from the porch. He only had eyes for Talia, though.

She walked slowly on her father's arm, wearing her mother's wedding dress and carrying yellow daisies. He was certain she had to be the most beautiful bride in the history of the world—about to make him the happiest man in the history of the world.

Talia glanced at her father.

He smiled wistfully back, whispering, "Happy, baby?"

"The happiest," she murmured, giving his arm a little squeeze.

Then she looked past the seated guests to where Cade was standing. Seeing him waiting there for her made her feel like a princess in a fairy tale. She'd fallen in love with the man of her dreams, and he'd fallen in love with her. And she truly believed in happily-ever-afters.

Ahead, her attendants stopped and moved to one side. A moment later she was standing in front of Cade. The look of love in his eyes brought tears of happiness to hers.

Her father gently kissed her cheek, then stepped aside as Cade took her hand.

"Dearly beloved . . ." the minister began.

"I'll love you forever, Talia," Cade whispered so quietly only she could hear.

"Me, too . . ." she whispered back. Their happily-ever-after had begun.

COMING NEXT MONTH

#365 NO ORDINARY MAN by Suzanne Brockmann
Dangerous Men

All single mom Jess Baxter knew about her new tenant
Rob Carpenter was that he had nice eyes, traveled a lot, liked
Chinese takeout—and was the sexiest man she'd ever met. But at
the same time he moved in, a stalker preyed on women in the
Florida coastal town—and Jess fit the description. Had she fallen
in love with a killer?

#366 THE CHARMER by Leona Karr
Avenging Angels

Ever since an "accident" temporarily took single mother
Shanna Ryan's eyesight, both a little guardian angel and sexy
Dr. Jay Harrison had been operating as her eyes. And Shanna needed more protection than she knew—because she and her daughter
had been targeted by a killer!

#367 THE OTHER LAURA by Sheryl Lynn

A bullet wound put Laura Hudson into a coma—and when she
awakened with amnesia she was sent to a ranch she didn't remember, to recover with a daughter and husband who hated her. But as
her husband began to fall in love with her again, she began to doubt
that she was Laura Hudson at all....

#368 THE PIRATE GHOST by Laura Pender
Dreamscape

For centuries Gabriel Dyer lived beneath the sea—until one night
when he rescued a drowning Tess Miller. Later, when Tess was
accused of murder, it was clear that the pirate ghost wanted to help
clear her name. But did Gabriel love Tess, as he claimed...or merely need her to avoid returning to his watery prison?

AVAILABLE THIS MONTH:

MILLION DOLLAR SWEEPSTAKES

Fall in love all over again with

This Time... MARRIAGE

In this collection of original short stories, three brides get a unique chance for a return engagement!

- Being kidnapped from your bridal shower by a one-time love can really put a crimp in your wedding plans! *The Borrowed Bride*— by **Susan Wiggs**, *Romantic Times* Career Achievement Award-winning author.

- After fifteen years a couple reunites for the sake of their child—this time will it end in marriage? *The Forgotten Bride*—by **Janice Kaiser**.

- It's tough to make a good divorce stick—especially when you're thrown together with your ex in a magazine wedding shoot! *The Bygone Bride*— by **Muriel Jensen**.

Don't miss THIS TIME...MARRIAGE, available in April wherever Harlequin books are sold.

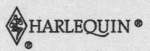

HARLEQUIN ®

Angels should have wings and flowing robes—not tight black jeans and leather jackets. They should be chubby cherubs or wizened old specters—not virile and muscular and sinfully sexy.

But then again, the AVENGING ANGELS aren't your average angels!

Enter the Denver Branch of Avenging Angels and meet some of the sexiest angels this side of heaven.

Sam—THE RENEGADE by Margaret St. George
(#358, February)

Dashiell—THE IMPOSTOR by Cassie Miles
(#363, March)

and the littlest angel-to-be
Ariel—THE CHARMER by Leona Karr
(#366, April)

Kiel—THE SOULMATE by Carly Bishop
(#370, May)

They may have a problem with earthly time—but these angels have no problem with earthly pleasures!

HARLEQUIN®

I N T R I G U E®

Sometimes a man is so magical, a day so unusual, a mystery story so strange that you're sure you must be dreaming....

So, dream with Harlequin Intrigue—and escape into the landscape of the unusual with:

#368 THE PIRATE GHOST
by Laura Pender

Available in April 1996 wherever Harlequin books are sold. Watch for more Dreamscape titles—coming to you from Harlequin Intrigue!

Harlequin Intrigue—we'll leave you breathless!

Harlequin invites you to the
wedding of the century!

This April be prepared to catch the bouquet with
the glamorous debut of

*Weddings by
DeWilde*

For years, DeWildes—the elegant and fashionable
wedding store chain—has helped brides around the
world turn the fantasy of their special day into reality.
But now the store and three generations of family are
torn apart by divorce. As family members face new
challenges and loves, a long-secret mystery begins to
unravel…. Set against an international backdrop of
London, Paris, New York and Sydney, this new series
features the glitzy, fast-paced world of designer wedding
fashions and missing heirlooms!

In April watch for:
SHATTERED VOWS
by Jasmine Cresswell

Look in the back pages of *Weddings by DeWilde* for
details about our fabulous sweepstakes contest to win a
real diamond ring!

Coming this April to your favorite retail outlet.

WBDT

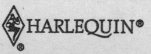

HARLEQUIN®

You're About to Become a *Privileged Woman*

Reap the rewards of fabulous free gifts and
benefits with proofs-of-purchase from
Harlequin and Silhouette books

Pages & Privileges™

It's our way of thanking you for
buying our books at your
favorite retail stores.

PROOF OF PURCHASE
H-PP118
Offer expires October 31, 1996

BONUS
Proof of Purchase
BHI-PP115
Offer expires October 31, 1996

**Harlequin and Silhouette—
the most privileged readers in the world!**

For more information about Harlequin and
Silhouette's PAGES & PRIVILEGES program call the
Pages & Privileges Benefits Desk: 1-503-794-2499

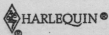

HARLEQUIN ®